Red Car

RED CAR

STORIES
SALLIE BINGHAM

Sarabande Books
LOUISVILLE, KENTUCKY

No part of this book may be reproduced without written permission of the publisher. Please direct inquiries to:

Managing Editor
Sarabande Books, Inc.
2234 Dundee Road, Suite 200
Louisville, KY 40205

Library of Congress Cataloging-in-Publication Data

Bingham, Sallie.
        Red car : stories / by Sallie Bingham. — 1st ed.
        p.   cm.
        ISBN 978-1-932511-59-8 (hardcover : alk. paper) —
ISBN 978-1-932511-60-4 (pbk. : alk. paper)
        I. Title.

        PS3552.I5R43 2008
        813'.54—dc22   2007022454

Cover and text design by Charles Casey Martin

Manufactured in Canada
This book is printed on acid-free paper.

Sarabande Books is a nonprofit literary organization.

THE KENTUCKY ARTS COUNCIL

The Kentucky Arts Council, a state agency in the Commerce Cabinet,
provides operational support funding for Sarabande Books with state tax dollars
and federal funding from the National Endowment for the Arts,
which believes that a great nation deserves great art.

For Francis

Contents

Acknowledgments

"Pleyben" originally appeared in *The American Voice*.

"Red Car" originally appeared in *The Beach Book: A Literary Companion*, edited by Aleda Shirley (Sarabande Books, 1999).

The quotation on page 99, and the story title "A Gift for Burning," are from the poem "Song" by Adrienne Rich.

Red Car

RED CAR

Car may not be the word. *Automobile* is long outdated and *car* seems to be going or to have already gone the same way, although it is perhaps still appropriate for this particular vehicle, a red '59 Cadillac convertible with a front seat wider than a porch swing, a cumbersome white top, and the makings of history in its various grills, bumpers, fins, and chrome ornaments.

To tell the story of this car is to tell the story of marriage; not their marriage, not the marriage, but marriage as it generally happens: a state, a place, a condition that gives rise to certain thoughts and attitudes, certain conclusions. Marriage equals the red car.

March: the red car has been parked for a year in front of a pretty frame house in Florida. It sits at the curb like a claim, loud

3

and clear, to the pretty frame house, an exclamation point in that quiet neighborhood.

The wife rode in the car for the last time in March. She had eaten dinner with her husband in a restaurant they visited on the way back from the airport, on the way to the airport, and often in between, a lively little place with a bar overlooking the ocean.

They both dreaded going back to the house. There's a silence particular to the end of a marriage, when there are no words, not even any actions to convey the despair, the listlessness, of the approaching end; and the broad white bed in the big bedroom is no longer even a hope or a possibility but another item on an endless list of disappointments and regrets.

So when he said, "Shall we take a drive?" she thought it was a good idea, to put off that end.

They drove out along the bay where the houseboats are snubbed up against the highway and the lights from the strip developments waver in oily darkness. He pulled her in under his arm and drove with his left hand and she wondered why, once again, she was allowing him to drive her when he was drunk, and why, once again, their past seemed to have returned: the one-handed driver, the broad seat, the woman shivering in a light cotton dress under the heavy arm of a man to whom she appears, against all reason, to belong.

They stopped to look out over the water for a while as, a few months later, they would stop in an overgrown field to look for the last time at a pair of circling hawks. The power that held them in the palm of its hand arranged these last times carefully: the beautiful golden field leading to massed sycamores at the edge of the creek, the beautiful expanse of the Atlantic at the edge of the built-up town. Last times have a certain weight, a smallness and density; they stay in memory, like pebbles at the bottom of a child's pail.

Driving back, she remembered the way the red car had come into their lives. A son, turning sixteen, bought it for one hundred dollars; the car barely moved, but the body was beautiful and the design recalled a vanished elegant life.

This son spent a desultory summer poking around under the hood with the help of a wisecracking handyman who knew something about machines. But the process was slow and before long the handyman had taken over; he knew what to do and he worked in the cool early morning before the young owner was stirring. So by the end of the summer the car was running, but it no longer belonged to the boy who had paid one hundred dollars for it. It belonged to the handyman's master, who had paid for parts and labor and who now had the car repainted a brilliant carmine red.

The boy did not protest when his stepfather took the car. After all, he had paid for the parts and the labor. The handyman drove the car down to Florida that winter and parked it in front of the pretty frame house.

As the marriage began to slide, the family seldom went to Florida; the trip was expensive in more ways than one, and no one hoped, any longer, to be able to enjoy spending time together. A few incidents had ended all expectation of that, substituting a brittle atmosphere where no one laughed or cried.

So the red car gathered dust and leaves outside of the pretty frame house. Passersby sometimes noticed it and wondered about its history.

In June the handyman's master, the husband and stepfather of the family, began to come down to Florida alone. He enjoyed driving the red car to restaurants, and when he met people there, he drove the car to their apartments. He liked to take the car that had been his stepson's (but not really) and in which his wife had sat, silent, under the weight of his arm, to little spots in Old Town, little apartments above bars, respites and hideaways where the young women who worked the bars and restaurants lived with their clutter of make-up bottles, their fleets of sandals, their blue jeans patched and faded, their collections of T-shirts, and here and there a snapshot of a mother back at home in Indiana.

Soon one of these young women laid claim to the red car. She had been taken to restaurants in it and she had put her comb in the glove compartment and her feet up on the seat as she curled in under the driver's arm. She felt sorry for him—another forty-ish married man who groaned when she stroked him—and she liked the car, and so one Sunday night when she drove him to the airport, she asked for the keys and he gave them to her.

Now she drove herself to work, parking the red car outside the clothing store where she was about to become assistant manager. It was hardly fitting for an assistant manager of a store that had outlets in Miami and Fort Lauderdale to come and go on a battered Schwinn.

After that the husband let the girl know what flight to meet on Fridays and she was always there, freshly showered, in a clean T-shirt and shorts.

It seemed a paradise, to both of them: the pretty frame house, paid for by the wife (who never came to Florida anymore); the pretty red car, which everyone noticed and admired, and which had belonged to the stepson (but not really), and the picture they made in it: the handsome fortyish husband and the girl who was assistant manager and knew her worst days were over.

The car seemed to lengthen; it seemed to take up more space at the curb.

Then one night there was trouble for the husband back East, and two men came down to Florida and began in an unobtrusive way to look for the red car. They were skillful professionals and no one would have noticed them except that their clothes were dark;

7

they did buy themselves "Last Plane Out" T-shirts but that did not blunt the edge of strangeness that made people look at them twice.

They went first to the pretty frame house. The car was not there, and the young woman, who by now was living in the house, did not appear to be there either.

They discovered the car parked in the bushes at the airport. They looked it over carefully and found a comb in the glove compartment.

Late one night they watched the young woman step off the Miami puddle-jumper and walk to the red car. She had a little suitcase which she threw into the back seat, and then she released the chrome hooks that held the top in place (with which the wife, who never came to Florida anymore, had often struggled) and pushed the top back. She pulled the car out of the bushes and started down the highway along the ocean, going at a good pace, and the two professionals drove along behind her.

First she stopped at a large expensive house and knocked on the front door. A Cuban woman (or so the professionals dubbed her) came out with a small child. All three got in the red car and drove rapidly to a pet store which, since it was night, was closed; however someone was waiting inside behind the bubbling fish tanks and the parrots on swings, and the three went in, emerging a few minutes later. They drove to another pet store on the other side of town and repeated the sequence. Then the young woman took the older woman and her child (if it was her child; the professionals couldn't tell, although she seemed protective of the little boy, holding him by the hand) back to the expensive house.

Next the young woman drove to an old house that was broken up into many small apartments. After she had been inside for a few minutes, a fancy foreign car drove up; the driver hopped out, went inside briefly, and came out again.

That was all that happened. Something had been claimed, exchanged, or given away; certainly, the professionals knew, money had been involved. But they couldn't find a reason to ask questions. Young women do come and go.

The red car, which had belonged to the sixteen-year-old boy, which had passed through the hands of the wisecracking handyman on its way to the fortyish husband who was about to become single again and in which he had driven his wife for the last time, was parked outside of an old house broken up into many apartments, where young women kept their clutter of make-up bottles, their fleets of sandals, their collections of T-shirts and here and there a snapshot of a mother at home in Indiana.

Did it all begin with the boy's silence when the car, as was only just, passed out of his hands? Or with the handyman's silence when the car, which he had fixed, passed along to the owner? Or with the silence of the wife when she sat under the weight of her husband's arm?

Red Car

Or is there another silence, the silence of night ocean and south wind, combing the darkness while these sleepers lie under the secret verdict of the future?

SAGESSE

In Normandy that summer just after the war, the weather was cloudy and gray. Sarah thought it matched the beach, which had suffered during the Invasion.

The new governess warned her, "Be careful, Sarah. You don't know what you might find. A boy digging in the sand blew his arm off."

"Blew his own arm off?"

The strange Mam'selle didn't smile. "He found a grenade, still lively." She seldom made a mistake in English but when she did, Sarah did not correct her. Mam'selle had been hired, Sarah knew, for the beauty of her French accent, which the three American children were meant to acquire during their summer abroad. Small mistakes in word usage did not matter.

"She's not a servant," Sarah's mother had explained, which

meant that Mam'selle was to be treated differently from the sighing cook at home in St. Louis, or the maid who made up their beds in the hotel.

Mam'selle came from a good family, had married into it, or was related in some other way. That family was gone, wiped out by the war, and so she was working as a governess for Americans. Sarah had learned this from her parents' conversation.

Her lost family had left Mam'selle a set of fine possessions. The possessions were few, but of the best quality; she carried them in a stout black leather suitcase, worn, but very clean. Its peach-colored silk lining smelled of sachet.

Sarah had looked in the suitcase cautiously when it was lying open on the foot of Mam'selle's bed. That was the first day of her employment, and she had been hanging the contents of the suitcase into the armoire, next to Sarah's and her two little sisters' clothes.

Mam'selle had arranged a series of peach-colored satin bags on the armoire shelves. What was in the bags Sarah didn't ask; instead, she studied Mam'selle's gestures, folding and tucking precious things away.

Sarah's family had brought eighteen pieces of luggage to France. When they traveled—and they traveled a great deal—all kinds of clothes were needed, as well as books, photographs of kin left back in the States, writing materials, and her mother's enormous dictionary.

Yet things didn't matter, Sarah thought, except for the moment when they were brought out of their boxes, smelling of newness. Soon enough, the girls' dresses, bought for the trip, the dolls, patent-leather slippers, and hair bows in every color lost their new smell and became encumbrances to be put away as quickly as possible, in the big armoire.

Mam'selle's things smelled of other times. The tiny gold binoculars (Mam'selle called them opera glasses), the soft long white gloves, the crisp black veil—all of them smelled of old times, sweet, if a little musty.

After Mam'selle had settled in, Sarah's parents left for Paris, and the three girls began to grow accustomed to the routine of hotel life.

Sarah ordered Sole Meunière every other night (every night, Mam'selle told her, would be extravagant), learned to drink bottled water instead of boiled milk, and ate hard-crusted bread with sweet butter that came in little pots.

On rainy days, they walked across fields to a farm where a woman gave them sour yogurt with a crust of cream at the top. Mam'selle and the woman talked, and Sarah began to pick up a few words of French.

On sunny mornings, Mam'selle took Sarah and her two little sisters to the beach. They were allowed to swim, but not to dig in the sand. Alice and Sarah wore dresses, at Mam'selle's insistence, with smocked bodices and puffed sleeves, which they had worn to the country club, back home in St. Louis.

The youngest girl wore a romper over her diapers and spent the morning lying on a shawl, protected from the sun by an open umbrella.

Mam'selle arranged their things in neat piles—sandals, sailboats, pails, and towels—near the slatted wooden dressing hut the parents had rented for the season.

Later, inside the hut, Mam'selle helped the girls change into their bathing costumes (as she called them) under their dresses. At first Sarah protested, but then she became interested in the way this was accomplished.

First, she stepped into her damp woolen bathing suit and pulled it up over her thighs, under the full skirt of her dress; and then, Mam'selle lifted the dress over her head while Sarah, at exactly the same moment, pulled the bathing suit up to her chest. Finally, she slipped her hands through the straps as the dress flew off.

At the end of the morning, the whole process was reversed, which meant, Mam'selle explained, that Sarah and her sisters did not have to submit to the indignity of wearing wet sandy bathing costumes when they walked up to the hotel for lunch.

Something precious was being protected in this way.

Sarah was reminded of the saint's thighbone that lay inside a gold box in the village church. On special days, Mam'selle told her, the box was taken out and paraded through the streets, but it was never opened. No one would have been equal to the sight of the naked bone.

Mam'selle did not possess a bathing costume. On the beach, she wore one of her black dresses, which were not quite uniforms—there were differences in detail, a lace collar, an embroidered yoke. When they came back from the beach, she took off each laced-up black shoe and shook out the sand.

Sarah was embarrassed by the sight of her feet, curled like kitten paws inside her black stockings.

At meals, Mam'selle taught Sarah a few more words of French. Her sisters were too young to take an interest, but Sarah practiced her new words on the waiter, redheaded Eduard, who laughed, and on the mouselike maid, Henriette, who did not seem to understand.

Eventually Sarah learned what to call the articles in the bathroom she shared with her sisters and Mam'selle, a room as dark as a chapel. *Comb*, she would say, *brush*, and think of the governess's thick braid of black hair, which she let down every evening.

Mam'selle taught her how to differentiate between the other children and their governesses at the hotel. Sarah might talk to the English and the French, but never to the German. There were only two Germans, a sad-looking elderly lady with a dispirited boy, who sat in a remote corner of the big white dining room.

Red Car

One morning at the beach when Alice was playing at the edge of the water and the baby was asleep on her shawl, Mam-'selle began to talk about her life. Sarah was an eager listener, and after that Mam'selle always talked to her when the younger children were out of the way.

First, she told stories about her childhood in the precious time before the war.

In her village, there had always been enough to eat—this was a cardinal point.

Then there came a shady period when Mam'selle said she had been "moins sage." Sarah thought she meant the herb they used at home with roast chicken, pronounced oddly. At that time, Mam'selle confessed, she had gone about the streets in short skirts.

But at last in a blaze of light and white lilacs, she was married, and spent happy years in a city in North Africa where her husband pursued his military career.

With the war, shadows and silences fell. It was not only the defeats, the deaths, although Mam'selle told Sarah about all of them, omitting no detail. It was what she called "the loss of heart."

Sarah began to mourn then for something she had never known: Mam'selle's youth, blown up to the blue North African sky along with sand and buildings.

As to what had happened to her young husband, Mam'selle indicated that he had been killed in one of the early engagements.

"One must go on," Mam'selle said at the end of the story, stretching her black skirt over her knees.

When Sarah asked questions, Mam'selle became discreet or distracted. So the stories lacked the explanations Sarah was used to from the time her mother had told her about the three little pigs; here was no straw house, to be seen as a symbol of the pig-builder's laziness, no brick house, proof of his brother's foresight. There were only the stories themselves, endlessly unfolding.

The evenings were long after Alice and the baby were asleep and Mam'selle retired to the bathroom for her ablutions. Usually Sarah lay on her bed, reading books her father sent down from the British bookstore in Paris. There were novels about the Crusades, and Robin Hood, and one about Saint Joan and her great war.

One dismal afternoon when they were walking back from the yogurt farm, Mam'selle took a short cut through a park, as she called it. It was not a park in Sarah's view but a vast lawn leading to an empty gray castle. The Germans, Mam'selle said, had pillaged it, and the family no longer came.

At the edge of the lawn, they saw a small chapel with a stained-glass window that showed a woman holding a lily and a shield. The door had been forced, and Mam'selle allowed Sarah to step inside.

Under the stained-glass window, there was a stone tablet on which two names and four dates were carved.

When Sarah called out the dates, Mam'selle explained that

they recorded family deaths: two generations, father and son, had been killed fighting for France. Sarah read the inscription aloud—"Mort pour la France"—and looked at the stained-glass lady with her lily and her shield.

On the way back to the hotel, they passed another engraved stone tablet, set into a wall. Mam'selle explained that it commemorated another kind of death, at the hands of a German firing squad. "We were not all shameless," she said.

On their next visit to the yogurt farm, Sarah realized she could understand some of the conversation. The farm woman, hands stuffed under her apron, was telling Mam'selle about a child, or children, who had spent the war years hidden in the hayloft.

Mam'selle listened without comment. At the end of the story, she embraced the farm woman with unusual warmth.

And then a great weekend arrived: the parents were coming down from Paris. Alice, waiting, ran back and forth to the hotel's front door. Sarah waited more discreetly. When the parents finally appeared, with boxes of presents and suitcases, life began to move.

Bicycles were rented in the village, and everyone except Mam'selle rode them to see a nearby castle, not the gray empty castle in its park, but one with furniture, and a guide. In the evening, Sarah's father started a new book for her by reading its first chapter aloud; it was about a Frenchman who went to America to fight in the Revolution.

But what Sarah remembered most clearly from the frantic two days was a moment with her mother in a roadside flower garden. Her mother insisted on stopping the car, and in her limited French, she asked the man hoeing there if she could pick some flowers. They were orange and pink nasturtiums, and when Sarah smelled them, she remembered that her mother had a row of nasturtiums outside the side porch at home.

"Are you homesick?" her mother asked when she noticed Sarah's face. "Do you want to go back to St. Louis?"

"No," Sarah said. "I'm learning French."

In September, after most of the other guests had left the hotel, Sarah finished the last novel in her father's box, a romance about the days of the knights.

She went to Mam'selle, who was sitting on the bathroom stool, holding Alice on her knees.

"I want to be honorable," Sarah said. "Like the knights, fighting for something."

Mam'selle took her request to heart and meditated on it while she waited for the thermometer in Alice's mouth to register.

"You will face challenges when you are older," she promised. "Now it would be wise for you to get a little air."

Sarah was never allowed to go out of the hotel alone, but now Mam'selle wanted her to walk to the village to pick up some medicine the doctor had prescribed. Alice was not gravely ill but she had a cough that made the doctor frown.

Mam'selle folded up several Francs in a piece of paper and put it in Sarah's hand. "Go to the pharmacy and come right back," she said, in French; by now Sarah could understand every word she heard.

She felt important and serious as she started out, her old winter coat buttoned to the chin.

Walking along the seawall, she watched the curl of low waves as they broke over debris left in the sand. Further along, she passed the smashed concrete bunkers the Germans had built, their evil eyeholes aimed at England. She hurried past those dark openings.

When she reached the village, she stopped to look at sailboats in the toy shop window, then hurried on, remembering she was too old for such things.

At the pharmacy, she handed paper and money to a man who stood above her, behind a high desk. The man smiled at her, and gave her change in thin coins she couldn't count.

Going back along the seawall, she noticed a ray of sun on the water and decided to walk the rest of the way on the beach.

As she walked, she saw a boot in the sand. It looked almost new, and it was still laced to the top. She turned it over; the other side was torn out. She wondered if the sea had done that, grinding the boot against a rock. Or perhaps an exploding shell had shattered it, and the foot of the soldier; but why was the boot still laced?

She hurried on.

Three men were approaching her from the other end of the beach. She walked with her eyes on the tips of her shoes, her hands in her pockets.

The men passed quite close to her, and then one of them said something, and she felt a hand reach under her coat and skirt and touch the back of her naked thigh.

She slipped quickly away.

As she ran, she stumbled over more debris—rusted chunks of metal, and wire caught up in tattered cloth.

In the hotel lobby, she stopped to catch her breath. The concierge behind his desk was watching her.

Then she climbed the two flights of stairs to her room and went in and lay down on the bed, without taking off her coat or emptying the sand out of her shoes.

After a while she remembered Alice's medicine and carried it to Mam'selle. As she handed her the medicine, Sarah apologized for taking so long.

"I know you were wise," Mam'selle said, looking frightened. She used the French noun that sounded like the herb.

Sarah looked at her shoes.

"Why are you sad?" Mam'selle asked.

"I'm always sad after I finish a book," Sarah said, in French. It was her first whole sentence.

Then, in spite of herself, she began to cry. "There is no honor," she sobbed.

"It is the war," Mam'selle said.

"But the war is over," Sarah said in French, using words she hadn't known she knew.

"You are speaking French," Mam'selle said.

That evening after Alice and the baby were put to bed, Mam'selle took out a crochet hook and a ball of silky white thread and showed Sarah how to make the chain stitch.

As she worked, Mam'selle talked about her wedding dress, which she had sewn herself in the town in North Africa, crocheting lace onto a hem that swept the ground.

"We thought it would be all right, after the war," she told Sarah, "after the Americans came."

Then she added, quickly, "At least now we can eat. Do you understand what that means, Sarah, you who have never been hungry?"

"Yes," Sarah said, "but it is not all right, and it is not going to be all right."

Mam'selle was silent, pressing the point of her crochet hook into another knot of white thread.

Then the hotel was emptying, and it was too chilly to go to the beach. The parents came down to take the children to Paris; they had found the perfect house.

Mam'selle was packing her black suitcase when Sarah went to tell her the news. "Five bedrooms," she said, "which means a room for each of us."

"I will be returning to my village," Mam'selle said, and now she spoke the frozen English of their first weeks together. "It is better so."

"It is not better so!" Sarah cried, and she ran to her mother to demand an explanation.

When she saw her daughter's flushed face, her mother shook her head. "You must learn to control yourself."

"But why——?"

The head shaking continued, the slight motion like the one used to shake salt over food. When Sarah continued to demand, her mother said, "Mam'selle was all very well for a summer vacation, but not for Paris. She is not suitable."

Walking back along the hotel corridor, Sarah remembered the short skirts Mam'selle had worn at the time when she had been "moins sage." That adjective was not yet in Sarah's vocabulary, but she knew it had something to do with the war, something shameful, like the touch of the man's hand on her thigh.

Red Car

When everything was packed up and loaded into the car, Mam'selle gave Sarah the little opera glasses. "Everything will all be right in time," she said, "when the years pass."

And then she was gone, with a small flourish of her gray skirt as she climbed into the car.

PLEYBEN

The woman in the hotel doorway seemed suspicious, almost hostile, as though she expected the two people to force their way in under her arm. She was holding open the glass door, and the tiles in the entry, moss-green, gleamed in the first sun they'd seen all month.

In crippled French, Lovett asked for a meal, and explained why they were so late: the road, the car breakdown, the sudden deluge of rain, which they had come to accept as part of the landscape of Brittany.

The woman either understood or didn't. In any event, she stepped back and let them inside.

The entry was damp, with a smell of old cooking. They took off their soaked raincoats and hung them on a pair of hooks. Mrs. Lovett was afraid of the pools of water which began at once to gather beneath the coats; she drew the woman's attention to them in English, which was the only language she knew.

The woman shook her head and hurried away, presumably to find some rags.

"Shouldn't we wait and help her clean up?" Mrs. Lovett asked.

"Let's go ahead and sit down," her husband said.

They went through another door into a small dining room, set against the outside wall of the large old building; the street was level with the windowsills, which were decorated with boxes of plastic geraniums. On the other side of the street, in an expansive flash of sun, the cathedral they had just visited turned its broad flank.

"I didn't like that bone place," Mrs. Lovett said as her husband pulled out her chair.

"The ossuary," Mr. Lovett corrected her, setting the word between them and what they'd seen. The smell of old bones had been as palpable as the steam from a bowl of chicken soup, magnified by the damp. There had been something matter-of-fact about the place: a kitchen where Death cooked, then stored its food.

They were alone in the dining room, because of the hour; in any event, Pleyben was not a place for tourists. Several tables were still littered with crumbs and crushed white napkins, with empty wine bottles in the center, like shrines.

Lovett consulted the menu, which looked entirely unfamiliar.

They had been staying on the coast, and had learned the names of various seafood there, but this menu did not offer *fruits de mer*.

Mrs. Lovett was still thinking about the bone place. She had a habit of dwelling on a subject, like an oyster coating a grain of sand. "I can understand the logic of it," she said, placing her big purse on the table. "In these old graveyards, there isn't room to let everybody lie forever. But why keep the bones at all, I wonder? Why not just throw them out or burn them, when the grave is needed for someone else?"

Lovett was still looking at the menu, searching for a familiar word. He wished for their friends from the coastal hotel, a pair of touring Englishmen who had taught them about the local food and wine, taught them without a hint of condescension, too. "I think this is a kind of vegetable soup," he said, showing his wife the name on the menu. "Let's start with it."

"I'm chilled to the bone," she said, suddenly, her voice darkening, and he looked at her, uneasy as he always was when she changed her tone.

"You need some good hot soup, and a glass of wine," he said.

The woman who had let them in now reappeared. She stood over Lovett, waiting for his order. Under her frown, he broke down and simply pointed to several items on the menu. He realized how tired he was, how the month of travel had worn away his resolve to enjoy himself.

"She'll have the same thing," he said, gesturing at his wife. The woman seemed to understand. She went away briskly, with a sense of mission.

"I hate it when you do that," Mrs. Lovett said. "You didn't even bother to ask me what I wanted."

"I can't cope with the menu. Half of it is handwritten, and I can't make it out."

"Sorry," she said, reaching across the table for his hand. "My, your hand is cold. Nobody warned us about all this mist and rain."

"We wouldn't have listened to them, anyway," he said, brightening. He wished there was some way to fix her as she was now, her face losing its obscure, shadowed pallor.

The woman reappeared with a large white tureen. She set it down on the table and removed the cover; steam rose from its watery contents, in which several large pieces of bread floated, as well as a few carrots. Lovett seized the big tin spoon and began to serve his wife. "I imagine this is real local food," he said, and told the woman, this time in practical French, that they would have a bottle of red wine.

Watching his wife spoon the thin gruel, and then take a sip of the wine the woman had poured, Lovett thought he could see health and hope flooding back into her face. She sighed and pushed her chair back a little, and he knew she was spreading her knees under her skirt.

28

"I feel better now," she said. "That bone place did get me down."

"Ossuary. I would have avoided it, but I didn't understand the sign."

"We've certainly seen enough graveyards, this trip," she said cheerily, "and they really don't bother me at all. But something about all those bones—"

"Don't think about it," he said.

That held them silent for the next few minutes, while they finished the soup and their first glasses of wine.

Lovett had never before felt such urgency for food and drink as he had these last weeks. It seemed that he and his wife traveled along a line slung between meals, a line that sagged badly midway. He did not think of himself as a glutton or a drunkard, yet on several evenings he had fallen into bed dead drunk, waking up to his own loud snores as, earlier in the summer, he had sometimes woken up to his wife's sobbing. And his stomach was always full, too full, shoving his belt.

By the time the main course came—a sort of pot roast, with vegetables around it, succulent as a steak would have been at home—Mrs. Lovett could no longer be put off. She was determined from time to time to talk because, she said, she felt in that way she might stave off nightmares. It was the nightmares that left her sobbing.

"I wish now we'd had her cremated," she said, softly and carefully, cutting a bit of meat.

"Why?"

"Then I wouldn't have to imagine things. I'm sorry, George."

"Don't be sorry. What things?" He knew he had to ask.

"What's happening to her now, underground."

"Nothing is happening," he said, taking a mouthful of wine.

"But it's bound to. They can't stop it."

"You remember what the mortician said about the coffin." He nearly choked on a piece of dry bread. "He said that coffin is designed to hold out ground water for a hundred years."

"I think that's just talk," Mrs. Lovett said. "I bet it doesn't hold a month. Once wood is underground, it starts to rot—you know that."

"But it's treated," he croaked. "They explained that."

"I don't believe it," she said.

"Why think about it?"

"I can't help it. Sometimes I wake up feeling as though I'm in there with her, and I can see and feel what's happening to her."

"She's gone, she's not in there," he said.

"But then where is she? I know her only in that body," Mrs. Lovett said.

Mr. Lovett turned his head and looked out the window at the broad side of the dark old cathedral. A cloud was passing over the sun now, and as light drained from the stone walls, they darkened as with a stain. It would begin to rain again soon, he thought, and wondered why he did not find the prospect daunting. Everything fit, this time, as it had never fit before: his wife's voice, the cathedral walls, the gathering clouds.

"Look, you can see the calvary from here," he said, almost exulting. "There's the thief who wasn't sorry, with his tongue stuck out. Did you notice, there's a little horned devil, like a toad, sitting on his shoulder?"

Mrs. Lovett leaned across the table. "I remember the way her little limbs used to feel when she was a baby, so smooth and pliable. Sometimes it seems to me they must be that way again, just so smooth and soft. I know it's terrible to talk this way."

"Tell me, if it helps," he said, but now he knew that was not his reason for listening.

"I'm ashamed," she said. "It's almost obscene."

Yes, obscene, he wanted to shout with a great laugh, a belly laugh, his mouth full of red wine that would spray across the table, soaking her white blouse.

"Father Bill tried to get me to put it all out of my head," she continued, "to think about Katy's spiritual life. I don't think she had a spiritual life. I think she only had the life of the body. So now when I think of her, I think of the way her body is going on, underground."

He got up and came around the table, then squatted awkwardly by her chair, as he had done on many other occasions when she had hastily burst into tears. This time she did not cry.

"I want to think about it from beginning to end," she said. "From her warm little body when she was first born and they laid her on my belly to her warm little arms and legs when she'd been playing in the sun, her warm round nakedness when she was still young enough to go swimming without a suit, and then all of a sudden her little round breasts and that time you said she was too old to wear a T-shirt without a bra."

"Forget that."

"And the time I felt her leg after she'd shaved it, and it was as smooth as glass, ankle to thigh."

"How does all that connect?" he asked, not looking at her for fear she would see his avidity.

"I think she's still growing. Her hair and fingernails, of course. But something else, too. The cells. I think the cells are growing down there in the damp. The skin cells and the ones inside that would have turned into babies."

Lovett stood up. "We're getting out of here," he said.

"But we haven't even had our dessert." Still, she followed him when he went out into the entry, cornered the dour woman, and paid for their meal without waiting for change. The same urgency that had filled his mouth with wine was driving him, again, driving him to hear his wife, to take in her words. He hurried her out to the car and packed her inside.

Then he climbed in and wrenched the car into reverse, wheeled backward down the cobblestones and turned to follow the arrows that pointed toward the road to the coast.

"Tell me some more," he said.

Now she was prim, almost angry. "I don't understand. It's very unpleasant. Why do you want to hear it again?"

"I can't feel anything about her," he said. "I've tried imagining the way it happened, the motorcycle, but I can't get anywhere. Maybe if I start where she is now and work back—"

"Why should you want to? You never wanted to, before," she said, as though she saw the face of greed or lust, like the face of the little horned devil perched on the shoulder of the unrepentant thief.

"It's terrible that it happened, but somehow it's worse that I can't feel it," he said, and pulled over to the side of the road and rolled down his window. The smell of a crushed herb of some kind filled the car, and the sun, for a moment, glared down on the sodden gray-green hills. "Help me feel it," he said.

"I can't do that," she said, shrinking into the corner of the car.

He took her hand and kissed it. "Please."

She said carefully, "I think maybe all that matters is she died."

Lovett was silent.

33

"Why don't we drive on? I know you want to get back to the hotel in time for drinks with those nice Englishmen."

He reached for her then, reeling her in, and pressed her head against his lapel as though to comfort her; but she was dry and still. He wanted to put his face down inside her blouse, to feel her heart beating there under her thin, cool skin.

ADVANCED LATIN

While she talked, Luke watched the sun glint on the cars in the parking lot and, further off, the snow on the Sangres turning red. It was rush hour and the highway that passed the shopping center was thick with cars.

She'd come in an hour earlier, to take her first lesson—he offered two trial lessons for fifteen dollars, losing money on the deal but catching a few permanent clients—and now she was telling him she wanted to learn how to dance because of how she used to live.

Horses, he heard, and children, and knew that meant a big house somewhere and a husband who would never be mentioned, or if so, just to laugh.

Across the parking lot, he noticed a woman in a short skirt and tall black boots walking away from her car. She had the thighs of a dancer and he wondered if she was coming to his studio. But she turned left at the last minute and went in the sporting goods store. It didn't matter; these days, he had plenty of customers, and some of them had even better legs.

Meanwhile Mrs. Lewis went on talking about dancing as a girl at parties given by her parents and their friends. She didn't call them debutante parties but he knew that was what she meant. He had several customers practicing waltzes for just such occasions.

Finally he made her sit down next to him on the bench that ran all the way down the long wall of his studio, under mirrors that had cost almost as much as the floor. The bench was padded with blue acrylic and it opened, in sections, for storage. There were old dance shoes in there, bits of rainbow-colored costumes. Once a year he opened the benches and threw everything out.

"This is the way we do it," he said, and he showed her several lesson plans. Johnny, his floor manager, thought it was better not to show them the options in writing, but Luke knew they never read the contracts anyway. They rode along on his voice, waiting for a chance to sign.

The dance lessons were sold in blocks of ten, twenty, or more, and they were expensive, especially if the woman wanted to work with Luke. For the others teachers, the charge was less, but it all added up to a substantial amount, paid for on the spot, in advance, by check.

Mrs. Lewis took a check from her purse and wrote out the larger sum and he saw she wasn't going to make a notation on her stub. In fact she didn't have a stub. The check had been loose at the bottom of her alligator-skin purse.

"When do I start?" she asked, her face lifted up to him, as though he was going to shine on her, or rain.

"Tomorrow, two o'clock," he said, checking his schedule.

"I only know a few steps from parties. Jitterbug, mainly."

He'd noticed, dancing with her, that she held herself badly, back arched, shoulders up, head too far forward. The tall ones usually did.

"That doesn't matter," he told her. "I'll start you over, from scratch."

She smiled. "Daddy danced with me every evening for a week, trying to teach me the waltz so I could get married. But he decided it was impossible. Or I was."

He imagined her father's arms, the cut of his suit. So many women were taught to dance by their fathers, and then came to the studio to be fixed.

"Did you waltz at your wedding?"

"Yes—no way out. We stepped all over each other, and I ended up crying."

He liked her face, its brightness, the worn skin covered with a skillful layer of make-up. He liked it when the older ladies made an effort, wore the right kind of shoes, and short skirts, if they had the legs.

"Tuesday at two o'clock," he said, writing her name on his appointment sheet.

During her second lesson, it began to rain and he wondered if he'd remembered to close his car windows. It was a secondhand Chrysler with 52,000 miles on it, but the previous owner had kept it in good shape. He sent Johnny to check. Johnny came back running because it was raining harder now. He said the windows were closed tight.

Luke nodded and went on teaching Mrs. Lewis the rumba which was the way he usually started them to see if they could move their hips, or learn to. She laughed when he called it Cuban Motion, but then she tried to mirror the motion he was making, drawing in at the waist and releasing one hip smoothly, and then shifting to the other side. She had some flexibility in her long torso, which he could see because she had worn a leotard. He thought she might have gone out earlier in the day when the sun was still shining to buy the leotard and the short flared skirt that was like the ones his women teachers wore.

He put his hands on her waist, and then slid them down to her hips. It was the first time he'd touched her and she stood for it patiently. No woman ever objected in words to being touched, but some of them reared back. He remembered his mother warning him against touching girls and wished she could have lived to see his studio, bought with a big bank loan he was now paying off, five instructors instead of the two he'd started with, and Johnny to take care of the business end.

As he counted out the beats, he felt her moving her hips more smoothly. He went to put a CD in the stereo, and when he took her in his arms again, he felt the difference that music nearly always made. The tune was an old one from the fifties and he knew she'd heard it at slumber parties and later at her first teenage dances.

She sighed. She wasn't doing the rumba anymore, but she was on time and enjoying herself and he didn't correct her.

"You move well," he told her. It gave him satisfaction to find that movement, that flexibility. He thought she might decide to really work at it, take more lessons, turn out to be serious. Those were the ones who paid the bills.

That evening when he was watching TV at home Pauline asked how the new one was doing and he said there were possibilities. Pauline had been his partner when he was performing, and she kept an eye on the women who came in.

A few months later he planned to take five of his most advanced students, or at least the ones who could afford it, to a competition sponsored by his old studio in Denver, and Mrs. Lewis—Cindy—decided to go along. She bought herself a couple of gowns from the one good dress store at the mall, and a week before the competition, she brought them to the studio and tried them on for Luke, running in and out of the bathroom, bra straps showing, wearing sneakers. He liked the turquoise-blue stretch but told her to take back the gray silk because it didn't move. He knew she was not the kind of woman who returned clothes and he thought the gray one would probably end up in the back of her closet.

At the competition, he was too busy dancing with the students to pay much attention to any one of them, so it wasn't until the last day, when it was all over, that he had a minute to sit down and chat with Mrs. Lewis.

She looked tired and her azure eye shadow was smeared up into her eyebrows. She was wearing the blue dress which she'd done quite well in——he reminded her of that——but she'd taken off her dancing shoes; her bare feet, in nylons, looked twisted, several toes turned under.

"I didn't do as well as I expected," she said. She was looking down at her coffee, turning the mug in her hands. "I let you down."

"You did exactly what you were supposed to do."

"Oh, why do you say that?" she wailed. "At least be disappointed."

Surprised, he took a sip of water. "But I'm not," he said.

"That's because you don't care," she said.

He wished Pauline was there, to put an arm around her shoulders.

"I do care," he said. "You have a lot of potential."

"You say that to everybody," she said. "I've heard you."

He sighed. It was late, the hotel coffee shop was empty except for a waitress swabbing the counter. The chandeliers overhead were lit with hundreds of little bulbs and the light shone mercilessly on her face.

"I want you to care," she said.

He told her it was time to go to their rooms—they were leaving early the next morning, in the rented van, to drive back to Santa Fe—and then he left to find the other instructors who were having a party on the twenty-fifth floor. All of Denver lay spread out beneath the windows and he wondered if things would be different in a big city like this one; then he remembered his days at the franchise and knew it was always the same.

Their own men don't do anything for them, he thought, standing at the window with a beer in his hand, but then, why should they? These women always leave.

On the way home in the van, Cindy barely said a word.

July Fourth was party-time at the studio and the staff worked late the night before, putting up red, white, and blue paper streamers and little American flags, in bunches. The big summer stars were all over the sky when Luke looked up, and their size and grandeur made him think of his father who'd never gotten around to applying for citizenship; the jobs he worked didn't require papers. When he turned sixty, he started drinking, and one night, late, he told Luke, "Your life will be nothing, like mine was, and you won't even have a good woman like your mother." Luke had told him that he was already making a better life, as a dance instructor at a big-city franchise, but his father had only laughed. Dance instructors, he said, were just toys for rich women.

Students sometimes contributed flowers or other decorations to the parties, and Luke was always quick to check the accompanying cards, in case there was one he needed to slip in his pocket. So when the balloon cluster arrived, butting in the doorway—six big heliums, red, white, and blue, with a basket of flowers attached by ribbons, underneath—Luke went right over. He had trouble finding the card lodged in the basket of flowers until Johnny pointed out the little envelope. Luke slipped the card out and read it, and then put it in his pocket.

Cindy Lewis wore a tomato-red dress to the party, with two thigh-high slits, and Luke noticed how much more muscular and shapely her thighs were, after six months of dancing, and also that she was wearing matching tomato-red silk underpants. He thought she had probably never worn red pants before, even for her husband.

"Thank you for the balloons and the flowers," he said, when

she asked him to dance a cha-cha. The balloons were lounging up near the ceiling, and the basket of red and white carnations bobbed by the dancers' heads.

"Did you read the card?"

"Of course. Thank you." His mother had died ten years ago, and his father, weeping, had said, "Now I have nothing." Luke had stood silent, his hands hanging by his sides, watching his father cry.

"I meant it," Cindy Lewis said.

"I know you did." Pauline had stopped sleeping with him at Easter, moving onto the sofa so she could have her space. Luke didn't know if she was going to change her mind; she'd done that two or three times. And the only independent studio in Albuquerque had just come on the market. Leasing it would mean running back and forth a lot in the car, but soon he would make enough money to replace the Chrysler with a Land Rover.

"Aren't you going to say anything more?" Cindy looked up at him with her damp, blue eyes, the lines like decorations, and he thought how pretty she was before he thought how pretty she must have been.

"No," he said.

"Oh, I know all the women are in love with you," she said, and then the cha-cha was over and he left her to put on a quick-step.

At the end of the party—he always ended them at nine-thirty, so people could go on to the bars and dance places around

43

town, where they could eat and drink and smoke cigarettes—she
came over to give him a hug and tell him goodnight. She'd already
taken off her dance shoes, and in her boots, they were exactly the
same height.

"I meant every word," she said.

"You can't send me notes like that," he told her.

"Is it against studio rules?"

She was smiling and twinkling, and the dampness was gone.
Now her eyes were expertly outlined with pencil and shadow.

"Yes," he said, turning away. Pauline, on the other side of the
room, was calling him to help close up.

"I won't accept that," Cindy Lewis said, behind him. He'd
known that was what she would say, that she would never accept
a rule she didn't want.

That night, in bed with Pauline, he thought about his father
saying that Luke would never have a life, or a woman as good as
his mother. He had a life but he was still in hock to the bank and
would be for years. His father had never believed a man could
make a decent living, teaching people how to dance.

He hated to have to sit down with Cindy and talk to her, but
he knew it had to be done. And at her next lesson, too.

It was a Wednesday, late afternoon, very hot; the studio door
was propped open, and the sweet, soft smell of gasoline and dust

drifted in. The air-conditioning was on the blink again, and people were complaining.

Cindy Lewis was wearing a short black skirt and a sleeveless leotard. She'd stopped wearing black tights since he'd recommended flesh-colored hose. When they sat down, the blue acrylic bench subsided a little, and Luke knew he needed to prop up that section. Something underneath was broken.

"I don't want to hurt you," he said.

"You're not hurting me."

"I mean, what I'm going to say."

"I know what you're going to say. Just don't say it."

"I don't need to?"

"No," she said, looking at him, and he saw she'd started to use maroon eye shadow with a pencil to match. "But I won't give up."

"You have to," he said. He felt as though he was trudging through mud.

"No, I don't." She spoke crisply, and he thought that was the way she must have spoken to her children, her horses, her employees. "It's a free country."

He trudged another step. "If you're going to keep on taking lessons. . ."

"Is it Pauline?"

"No," he said, heavily. "It's me."

"You think you have to earn everything, don't you," she said, and as she moved her arm onto the back of the bench, he smelled her deodorant, sweet and strong. "You think there's no free lunch."

"There is no free lunch," he said, and he thought of the franchise in Albuquerque, and the new Land Rover, with leather interior and automatic windows and a radio that could pick up stations as far away as Chicago.

LATER HE WOULD THINK, She broke me, but it was not as simple as that. In fact she went on taking lessons, five or six a week, and although Pauline was concerned about her—Pauline saw through people fast—Luke persuaded himself that everything was all right. Cindy didn't send him any more balloons, or flowers, or notes, and neither of them referred to the talk on the blue bench. Perhaps she'd decided it was hopeless, and was ready to concentrate on her dancing. That was all they talked about: her footwork, her frame.

In fact Luke was closer to several other students that summer, especially the married women who seemed securely moored. One of them, a handsome blond named Lucille who'd been coming to the studio for years, one of their bread-and-butter students who would never win competitions but would work hard and re-up every time their block of lessons was finished, came and told him—this was early fall—that a rumor was going around.

Luke was used to rumors—the business of dancing ran on gossip—and so he laughed and hoped she would not tell him. But she did. She was his friend, she said, and as his friend she thought he should know what was being said.

"I know already," he said, leaning down to tie his dance shoes; they were sitting on the blue bench, the one that caved in, and he reminded himself, again, to prop it up. "Either I'm sleeping with my students, or I'm gay."

"It's not that," Lucille said. "I wouldn't pay any attention to that kind of thing. No, they're saying you've got a problem with cocaine."

The word was one that had swung in and out of his life, like a moth attracted to a light and then disappearing. In fact it was a word he had almost never said, as though saying it would prove something. But he knew it.

"That's ridiculous," he said, "with the hours I teach." He was at the studio ten or twelve hours a day, first to arrive, last to leave, and sometimes he had to clean up, too.

Lucille just looked at him. She was a therapist, and he imagined she knew something about drugs.

"It'll blow over," he said.

"I don't think so."

"Why?"

"I'm hearing it everywhere."

He thought of Daisy Middleton bringing in her twelve-year-old daughter, a little fox in a skimpy dress, and then sitting on the bench to watch during the girl's lesson; that was one of their rules. Parents had to accompany minors. Daisy Middleton who'd told him she was pleased to find he ran a decent place. And all those physicists from Los Alamos who looked as though they'd never gotten dirt under their fingernails.

He asked, "Who started it?"—then suddenly knew.

She told him. "She swore me to secrecy—"

"She's mad at me," he said, as though that would solve it, end it.

"You've got to do something," Lucille said, and later, when he told Pauline, she said the same thing: "You've got to do something, Luke, you've got to stop it. It could ruin the business."

He remembered his father, then, with a spit of rage, as though his father, twenty years dead, had caused this to happen.

"I'll speak to her," he said.

"That won't do any good. She's already told a lot of people."

He knew then what he would have to do, and he armed himself for it, trying to imagine how his face would look to Cindy Lewis who suddenly seemed a stranger, although he had touched her everywhere and taught her everything he knew. He tried to remember how his voice sounded, in his own ears—his voice which his mother had always liked. But it was impossible to imagine it all because he could no longer see Cindy's face, which had been turned up to him, at the beginning, as though he was going to rain on her, or shine.

"I wonder how she came up with that," he said, in the dark, to Pauline, but Pauline, being wise, didn't answer.

The next evening when his ten or twelve best students—not the best dancers, but the ones who came a lot—were gathered for their Advanced Latin Class, he made them all sit down on the blue benches and settled himself on a little stool in front of them. He'd never seen the stool before, and he didn't know where it came from; he'd put his hand on it and known it was exactly right.

Sitting on the stool, he was a little lower than his students, and when he began talking, he found himself looking at their knees.

"There's a rumor going around. I want you, my core people, to stop it whenever you hear it. It could ruin me," he said, and suddenly, without knowing he was going to do it, he put his head down on his knees.

They sat studying him, silent as cattle.

He said a few things after that, and several seemed shocked or said they were sorry, but really it was all done when he laid his head down on his knees. In twenty years of teaching dancing— and there had been trouble before, of various kinds—he'd never done anything like that in front of his students, or his staff. In fact he'd never done anything like that in front of Pauline.

And still he hadn't been able to see Cindy Lewis's face, although she'd been sitting right in front of him.

They filed out, after his speech; no one said a word, as though they were the ones who were shocked, or frightened, or shamed. In the doorway, Cindy glanced back at him, with a little smile, and he thought she was pleased. She'd done it, now—brought down the house, or nearly, and he wondered if the same impulse had made her break her marriage, leave her husband, lose her children, shattering her own life as easily as she'd tried to shatter his, as though it was all paid for in advance, with no stub for the notation.

In the weeks that followed, no one canceled their lessons, and he never heard the rumor mentioned again—Lucille told him she hadn't, either—although now and then when he saw two of his women talking quietly in a corner, or crossing the parking lot together, deep in conversation, he suspected they were discussing what he'd said or what they'd heard, which began to seem like the same thing.

The danger passed, and everything went on in the same way, or would have if he'd let it go at that; but he found he couldn't face dancing with Cindy Lewis, looking at her averted face, knowing what she'd done.

And so he told her to leave. It was done quickly one evening in October. He had his checkbook out, and he wrote her a check for the lessons remaining in her contract, which she wouldn't be taking.

"I wish you the best," he said, holding out his hand.

"You can't accept anything, can you?" she asked. "I could have done a lot for you."

"I don't need you to do a lot for me."

"Oh yes, you do," she said, and then she was gone.

He stood watching her walk to her car; when Pauline called him, he turned around to get the students in Advanced Latin on their feet. But he could still feel Cindy Lewis striding away from him across the parking lot with her short skirt swinging as though she had indeed offered him something infinitely valuable—but what was it?

Pauline would say the moon.

DOING GOOD

Everyone in the courtroom—and there were quite a few, hangers-on as well as functionaries—tried to shield me from finding out what my son Hugh had done. I'd come straight from the airport and was still wearing my Cleveland disguise, which perhaps was the reason I was treated with deference, as though an odor of sanctity hung round me like a cloud of old-fashioned toilet water.

Even the social worker who had been assigned to Hugh's case minced her words. She was an attractive young woman with a clipboard, wearing what would have been called in the last century a riding skirt; I noticed these fashions had recently made a reappearance, even in Florida. When I'd bought the beach house, I'd thought I was escaping fashion.

She kept glancing at me during the hearing, when of course the details came out. "Hugh's been in fights before," I told her.

Red Car

The judge, a personable black man, seemed to feel responsible for the squabble that had caused Hugh to be ejected from the Green Parrot. He explained in an aside, spoken into the moist air but clearly intended for me, that vacationers don't always understand what he gently called the local mores.

I would have liked to sermonize on the national spread of these same mores but managed to hold my tongue.

Poor Hugh, whom I love more than anything on earth, sat in the dock with his beautiful blond hair drawn like a curtain over his face.

I've tried to tell him I have no quarrel with his choice. My father's best-looking and most energetic friends were invariably gay, and I spent my adolescence falling in love with them. Except for my determination to produce a son and a daughter—Hugh and his fascinating sister, Katie—I would have chosen such a companion myself. But thirty years ago, heterosexual husbands were the price we paid if we wanted offspring.

I find Hugh's lovers appealing. His trim young men remind me of those long-gone beaux of the forties, their custom-made uniforms and blazing insignia replaced by dangling gold crosses and inconspicuous tattoos.

Given all this, it galled me to be treated as though I was a stand-in for Mrs. Grundy. I do fit quite comfortably into my life in Cleveland, but that is a matter of sheer convenience. I don't waste energy on hopeless battles, such as integrating the Junior League or forcing my black friends to try to join the Country Club. This seeming indifference leads to misunderstandings.

After the hearing the lovely little social worker, whose name was Annie, brought me coffee and then steered me to a safe place in the crook of the outside stairs. The courthouse resembled a cheap motel—a long series of rooms connected by a balcony which lacked only umbrellas.

"I think your son will get off with a misdemeanor," Annie told me when she had me installed against a wall. "I wish my other clients were as lucky."

Instead of a diatribe on the injustices of the legal system, Annie then charmed me with a description of her latest case: Debra, a pregnant thirteen-year-old who had been interfered with by her father and was waiting court approval for an abortion. She even showed me a snapshot of the delicious girl, blond and pink in front of a matching hibiscus.

"Judge Thomas will grant her an abortion," Annie told me, "but the one free clinic here just closed. Their doctor was shot in the back. Debra's asked me to pay for her abortion, which of course I can't afford to do."

"If I provide money for this operation"—I rather enjoyed employing my mother's circumlocution—"I'll have to be responsible for everything that happens to her as a result."

"All it means is that Debra will control her own life."

"Control is harder to come by." I would have taken a byroad then and lectured about Fate, one of my favorite unfashionable topics, but the bailiff put his head out the door to say that Judge Thomas was back on the bench.

"Please think about it," Annie said, and I promised her to do so.

The State of Florida was represented in court by a gaunt-looking young man in work clothes and a tie, who seemed to have a good relationship with the judge, although what its nature was I couldn't determine. Annie whispered that he generally prosecuted with leniency, especially when a juvenile was concerned.

My son was represented by an older lawyer, dressed in wrinkled polyester and looking sizably bored.

This gentleman argued more persuasively than I'd expected that Hugh should be let off lightly, especially since the melee outside the Green Parrot, in which several garbage cans had been overturned, causing a neighbor to wake in alarm and call the police (a regular occurrence in that neighborhood), had caused no property damage or personal injury except for Hugh's bruised elbow, acquired when he had fallen among the cans.

"The young man is here for spring vacation," Hugh's lawyer explained, as though nothing more needed to be said. I remembered how Hugh's father had protested the notion of his seventeen-year-old son taking off (as Henry described it) for Florida on my money.

The State trotted out the obligatory horrors of late-night brawling, theoretical broken windows, and destruction of the citizen's right to undisturbed rest. The only note the State did not strike—and this, I'll admit, surprised me—was the one I'll call the Alternate Lifestyle. The fact that the Green Parrot is a gay bar—which had become clear earlier in the proceedings—and that the dispute prompting the bartender to ask my son to leave had something to do with jealousy among the regulars was not worth mentioning, in the State's eyes, persuaded me that something had changed in the State of Florida.

The verdict was swift. Again I noticed that Judge Thomas seemed chagrined, as though he expected me to take a bad account back to Cleveland.

I was hardly likely to do that since Hugh was let off with an entirely manageable fine and a lecture from the judge on the obligations of maturity. Even the demand for community work was dropped when I explained that I would be taking Hugh home, and safely out of the state, that night.

Hugh looked at me with a relief that nearly broke my heart. I have seen that look before. It doesn't presage conversion.

"I'll take you to lunch," I told Annie. "Perhaps you'll suggest somewhere with an ocean view."

She seemed astounded. "Don't you want to be alone with your son?"

It would have taken too long to explain that a private conversation was the last thing either Hugh or I wanted.

"Come along," I said, taking Annie's arm, and together we went to meet Hugh, who allowed me a kiss.

I find that with both my grown children "escapade" describes nearly all of their activities; a harmless sort of recklessness colors their lives. Unlikely as it sounds, their scrapes and scraps remind me of my mother's descriptions of her own green youth, when she would climb out her bedroom window to meet a suitor or offer her slipper as a receptacle for champagne. The true mischief in this world, of which there is plenty, is not done by these mild drifters; for them, reality remains just a distant comment on their lives.

Annie led the way to a pleasant terrace overlooking the sea, and we were installed under a yellow umbrella.

I am something of a gourmande (my size tells the story), and so I refused to begin a conversation until we had ordered: cold boiled lobster for me, with a dilled mayonnaise, and a hamburger for Hugh, who sticks to his carnivorous ways. Annie made do with a salad.

"How often do you weigh yourself?" I asked her, but I knew the answer already. She had had to exile her scale, she told me, like a bad dog.

"I starved until I was forty," I told her. "It didn't improve my life. Now I eat the best food money can buy."

Hugh looked at his lap in embarrassment. He is still trying to redeem himself from the misfortune of having been born to money, and likes me best when I put on a pair of old dungarees, tie my hair up in a bandanna, and go dig in the garden.

I was in my element. I loved the sea, the bright sun, the jaunty tilt of the umbrellas; I loved the look of young faces before everything would be altered by conversation.

Of course it had to begin, and so I began it. "As to your other client—"

"We don't need to talk about her, if you don't want to," Annie said.

"But I do want to. I think Hugh will find it interesting—" And I described Debra's predicament.

"Watch out, Mom," Hugh said. "Do you know what she wants?"

"Debra's confused," Annie admitted, not pleased by this turn in the conversation. "She's only thirteen."

"If I pay for this operation, I will have inserted myself into Debra's destiny, and I don't even know the child," I said.

Annie was shrewd. "You could meet her."

"I'm not sure I have the energy or the time," I said, to Hugh's scornful puff. "I think I like it best if she remains an abstraction."

Annie accepted this as an example of the slightness of my commitment. Still, she went on, "If you don't do anything, you're affecting her life, too."

Willy-nilly, I was caught in the toils. "Show Hugh the snapshot," I told Annie, and she dug it out of her purse. Hugh looked at it carefully.

"I always wanted another daughter," I mused, chiefly for effect. As soon as I said it, it became true—such is the power of words. My two guests stared at me in amazement.

"I know it sounds ridiculous," I admitted. "I'm fifty-five, far too old for an infant. I don't believe I'd stand a chance with the agencies."

"What about Father?" Hugh asked, looking alarmed.

"Your dear papa is hardly aware of what goes on in our house. It's very large," I told Annie. Hugh frowned. "Besides, he owes me a treat." I waited for Hugh to challenge me but he was chewing his hamburger and looking out to sea. "Trips to Europe and so forth don't really fill the bill," I continued, cracking one of my lobster's claws and extracting a delicate pink tentacle. "I need a New Interest in Life, as my mother would have said."

Annie hadn't touched her salad. "I don't understand."

"Let me put it simply. You've told me this girl has no family."

"She says they never want to see her again."

"I guess they're fed up," Hugh said.

"I think I would like, as the Famous Author said, to take up what has been cast off."

Neither Annie nor Hugh understood my reference. Hugh continued to work his way steadily through his hamburger but Annie was staring at me.

"Eat that wretched salad. You've thrown out your scale," I reminded her, and she took a dutiful bite.

"What are you willing to do?" she asked.

"Let me be perfectly clear. If Debra is looking for a home, I'll provide it, with or without her infant."

Annie said, "I can't really believe . . ."

Hugh explained, "Mom does these things. The house used to be full of strays."

"Animals, mainly," I reassured Annie.

"Debra is not a stray," she said.

"Of course not."

"I'm not sure it would be legal," Annie took another bite of salad without tasting it, I could tell.

She seemed to be fading away on me. "You'll have to supplement your diet with vitamins and minerals. I'll send you my regime," I said. "But first please check with the system and find out whether it permits a homeless girl to be adopted by a woman of means."

"She has some fairly serious antisocial behavior," Annie said.

"So have I."

Hugh laughed. "Mom does things to shock people, like taking home their silver candlesticks and sending them back a week later, gilded."

"Object stuff," I said. "It doesn't count. The only thing I really enjoy is messing with people's lives."

"I can see that." Annie was torn between dismissing me as certifiably mad and trying to milk me for the desired results. "Perhaps it would be simpler just to give Debra some money."

"I'm afraid it's too late for that. I'm already engaged in her life, as you pointed out."

Hugh said, "Mother never just writes a check. If they try to get her to give money to something like the ballet, she goes down and interviews the dancers first, and then there's a story in the paper about their ruined feet."

"That's only one example, and not a typical one at that," I reminded him. "Generally I deal in individuals, not organizations. The fraud in organizations, especially in the nonprofit sector, is beyond my ability to detect, while the fraud perpetrated by individuals is usually touchingly obvious."

Annie asked, "How in the world do you have the time?"

"I don't give dinner parties."

"Rescuing is Mom's hobby," Hugh said, and I realized for the first time that he was proud of me.

"I love you, too," I said, and ordered dessert.

When the strawberries and crème fraiche arrived (and they have no notion what crème fraiche might be, in those latitudes), I moved in to cinch the deal.

"We have about five hours till our flight," I told Annie. "If you want to pursue this, I'll need to meet Debra."

"She doesn't know what she wants," Annie reminded me, "and I'm not sure I can find her."

"Difficult, of course, on a Friday afternoon; but wouldn't she be at the beach?"

"I'll go look for her," Hugh said. I knew he'd wanted to go to the beach since he walked in the door of the Green Parrot. Much unacceptable behavior is simply a poor substitute for getting in the water.

"You know what she looks like from the snapshot; but how will you get her to come back with you?" I asked.

Hugh smiled. "I'll tell her she's won the lottery."

Even Annie, who was still looking very uncomfortable, had to laugh.

"We'll wait right here," I told him. Hugh bounded off and I ordered two espressos.

"Do you think you could get fond of this girl?" Annie asked.

"I don't know, and you wouldn't believe me if I pretended. All you have to rely on is my sense of moderation. I don't desire, and I don't rage. I'm nearly immune to disappointment. The worst thing that could happen is that she would be bored."

"Boredom wouldn't be the worst thing," Annie said. She smiled. I saw she was beginning to warm to my project, to see its possibilities.

Her smile made me hesitate. I hadn't counted on this being easy. "We can't make the decision for her. Debra may take one look at me and spit."

"Tell Debra what you're offering—if you know what it is—" (and of course I did not) "and then I'll tell her what her rights and responsibilities are, and she can decide. Are you hoping to adopt, if it can be arranged?"

"I won't abandon her, if that's what you mean. I don't get tired of people and drop them."

She didn't press me although I knew she would have liked to since she couldn't, understandably, believe me. I decided to be more explicit.

"I've lived for thirty years with a man I loved for perhaps the first six months," I told her. "I've gone through all the usual storms. Recently I decided to give up the house I love more than any place on earth. I am losing my son to something too vague to be defined. My daughter is already gone. None of this really amounts to anything, but perhaps it will give you some notion of my character."

"Where was the house?" Annie asked.

"On an island," I said. "South of here—a beautiful place. I nourished all kinds of illusions there."

She stirred her espresso in silence. After a while I asked her if she felt we had a tentative agreement. She said she thought we did—subject, of course, to Debra's reaction and the legal considerations.

"Won't your husband object?" she asked after a long silence during which she was possibly imagining Debra's good fortune and comparing it to her life as an ill-paid and overworked social worker.

"Henry wants me to be busy. It makes it easier for him to leave me behind. As for my children, they are both adults, or as adult as they are ever likely to be. They shared their childhood with my enthusiasms, most unwillingly. By now they've learned the situation's hopeless."

"I wonder what you'll think of her."

"I don't care what she looks like or how she slaughters the language or what disgusting personal habits she's picked up. I am taking her, as they say in another context, for better, for worse, for sicker, for poorer—"

"Nobody does that," Annie said, beginning again to doubt my sanity.

"They may have cut it out of the marriage service, its ghost still haunts," I said.

Red Car

Then I saw Hugh making his way between the tables. "I looked everywhere," he said, handing the snapshot back to Annie.

"I didn't expect you to find her," I said, and waved at the waiter for my check.

"I looked everywhere," he repeated, seeming so crestfallen I kissed him.

Annie sighed. "Of course it couldn't have worked."

"Who knows?" I asked as I paid, in cash; I can't bear the feel of those plastic cards. The waiter seemed nonplused and I explained that the bills were not counterfeit, simply new.

"You never meant to do it, did you," Annie said—she did not make it a question—as we were shaking hands.

"I suppose we'll never know. If Debra had appeared—"

Hugh said, "Mom, you know you would have taken her."

I think we all believed that, at least for the moment.

THE SHOT TOWER

All night long the state house floated, a lighted spaceship, on the other side of the acequia and what the orange juice king called PDP—Paseo de Peralta, the road around the old city of Santa Fe. In the early morning, the lights in the state house were extinguished by an unseen hand. Looking out the little window while she brushed her teeth, Janice wondered who was responsible, as she wondered who was responsible for the pale-yellow lady's shower cap (he always called his girlfriends ladies) that hung on a nail in the orange juice king's bathroom. It never occurred to her to ask; there are many things, she'd discovered in a long and varied life, that are better left to speculation.

They'd met six months earlier at a trailhead where they were both starting out to hike alone. He'd said she looked younger than she was, and that was enough to start things. The nickname she'd immediately bestowed on him, she realized now, had more to do with his ginger coloring than it did with his occupation, although he did sell fresh orange juice. It was the best orange juice in Santa Fe; there was nothing else in his two refrigerators.

"Not even milk?" she'd asked, a little dismayed, the first night she'd slept over—far too soon, she knew, but what could she do? It was the nineties, people didn't wait.

"Do you want milk?" he'd asked from where he was lying in the rumpled bed.

She was used to the accoutrements of sex, which sometimes seemed to be romantic love, or at least evoked it—its memory, very dim, its possibility, very remote: hot tubs scented with piney essences, champagne in crystal goblets, desolate drooping roses. The orange juice king had no accoutrements and did not seem to miss them. Instead he had a sense of humor.

After that they were seldom separated, except when he loaded his car with orange juice and delivered it to the coffee shops and health-food restaurants that anchored nearly every corner in Santa Fe. Then she went home to open her mail and check her messages; and, as spring passed into summer, the old adobe she'd bought to live in alone began to seem as remote as the artificial backdrop to a diorama—painted clouds and mountains.

In the hot days of early July, the orange juice king invited her to go camping overnight at Pecos, where a great forest stretched woolly and rustling over angular hills. Janice agreed right away although she knew she should have dissembled, invented other plans, been hard to persuade. The truth was she did everything he asked with a foolish madcap joy that made her grateful his requests were usually within reason. Lead me, she often prayed; Lead me, Oh Kindly Light.

The tarot cards had been favorable that morning, and she climbed into the orange juice king's battered car with her backpack and sleeping bag, feeling quite certain that for once in her life, fate was smiling. She'd turned up the Lovers card in a fortunate position, and she thought she knew the kind of union it predicted—uncertain, but full of illumination; even the telephone astrologist, whom she consulted in secret, had cried, "Go for it, Aquarius!" She was not used to such luck.

Riding along in his car, telling irrelevant, disconnected stories—she came from a line of storytellers, women variously stranded in fat, widowhood, or old age—Janice hardly noticed the transition from dusty desert to prickling mountain range. When they turned onto a dirt road marked, discouragingly, *No Campfires* ("But who would notice?" the orange juice king wondered), he told her in his abrupt way that he would have to leave her there for the afternoon; an emergency delivery of orange juice had been requested by one of his largest customers. He said he'd be gone a couple of hours.

Janice was not dismayed. In fact she was exhilarated.

They picked out a flowery uphill meadow, bordered with aspens whose shadows combed the long grass; pink clover was still in bloom, attended by bees and flies, and Julia saw a large monarch butterfly sitting on a purple nettle.

The orange juice king helped her to unload the car and set up the tent, and she was pleased when he told her he'd never used the tent before. Like the lady's shower cap in his bathroom, the big green tent might have been a symbol of repetitions. But it wasn't.

He did not have to drive back to town immediately, and so they lay down in the stuffy tent to nap. He wrapped her in his arms and fell at once into a deep sleep, as though he'd plunged into a well, while she lay smiling and dozing and rehearsing one of her grandmother's stories, aware meanwhile that her weight must be putting his right arm to sleep.

Sure enough when he sat up, it was "all tingly," as he described it. She reached to massage his palm, but he would have none of it, he was up and away. When he left her with a quick kiss, she knew she should have told him the legend of the old shot tower.

Lying on her back in the weeds, slapping ants, she told it to herself. Her grandmother, who'd been almost completely mired in respectability by the time Janice knew her, had told the story many times, always ending with, "I have the ring to prove it."

This is how the story went:

One spring day in Virginia, a young Confederate captain eloped with a neighbor's daughter his family opposed, for reasons lost in the mists of time. (That was one of her grandmother's favorite expressions.)

Crossing the fields on their way back from the secret marriage, they'd encountered a skirmish, and the young soldier-husband realized he'd have to hide his bride. He took her to an old shot tower, where hot lead for bullets was dropped from a platform twenty feet up into a shallow pool, the lead shaping itself perfectly along the way, and then hardening in the water. ("Ask me no questions and I'll tell you no lies," her grandmother had said when Janice questioned this use of gravity.)

The captain had helped his bride up the outside ladder to the platform, and then watched her climb down the inside ladder to the ledge that ran around the pool. She looked up at him, smiling, and said, "You have no reason to be anxious. I am perfectly comfortable alone."

Then the captain pulled up the inside ladder so no one could get at her, climbed down the outside ladder, and went to join his company.

The grandmother always paused dramatically at this point, and Janice, on her back in the weeds, paused dramatically, too.

"Now, it so happened," the grandmother's somber voice,

which had overtaken Janice's, went on, "it so happened that the young captain was grievously wounded in the skirmish, receiving a bullet in his head. He survived, but with no memory and few wits, living out the rest of his life as a doddering uncle, old before his time, in the family house.

"One day his nephew, who was a brain surgeon," the grandmother went on portentously (and now Janice was silent, on her back in the weeds), "his nephew decided to operate on the old man, to see if modern techniques could restore his mind. When the old man woke up after the operation, he stared around wildly, exclaiming, 'The old shot tower...I must get back to the old shot tower,' and they could barely restrain him.

"As soon as he was able, a great bandage still around his head, he rushed off across the fields with his family behind him." (Janice could see him, an ungainly figure loping along, the bandage coming undone and trailing.) "Inside the old shot tower, huddled on the ledge by the pool, they discovered a frail skeleton with a golden wedding ring on its finger.

"And that," her grandmother would always say, "is a true story. I have the ring to prove it."

For Janice, it had never been a satisfactory ending.

She got up to fix herself lunch. The camp stove was a spidery affair with three legs prone to collapse, and she was a little afraid of the butane canister with its many warnings. However, she assembled the stove on a flat rock, lit the flame, and began to heat some canned chili.

As she waited, she looked around the clearing where their bags and coolers and plastic containers of water were carefully arranged, and it seemed to her she had never been so at home as in this remote forest setting where she had no claim on anything, not on the shifting shadows, or the clouds, or the birds.

By the time she had eaten her lunch, savoring each bite of the peppery, oily chili, a cloud was looming over the tops of the pines. It had, she noticed, an oddly undefined shape, as though its aim was to take over the whole sky. A wind sprang up, moving stealthily toward her as though it, too, had a secret goal. Janice gathered up the bags and bottles and put them inside the tent.

When she sat down again, leaning against a pearly, scored aspen, her grandmother's story went on clanging in her mind. How could the girl—the bride—have allowed herself to be left in such jeopardy? Yet her grandmother said she had the gold ring to prove it, although of course a gold ring could prove anything, or nothing.

Perhaps, Janice thought, the bride decided she would as soon die if the captain didn't come back.

It was such an odd thought, unsuited to her life—several divorces, a son lost to chaos, more love affairs than she could remember, more moves and houses and jobs—that Janice wished the orange juice king was there, to make her see the humor in it. "Bog trotters always stay stuck in bogs," he'd say, or something equally satisfying; both their families were Irish.

She looked at her watch. He'd been gone two hours. She knew he usually underestimated the time a task would take—it was an aspect, she thought, of his eternal youth—and she imagined him back in Santa Fe, loading heavy cartons of orange juice into his car and delivering them to the Eat Your Heart Out Cafe, where he might stop to drink a cup of coffee and flirt with the waitresses. He had an abrupt, intrusive manner that startled women and disarmed them. "How are you?" he'd ask a young woman hustling by with a menu, and she'd stop and stare. Oh yes, Janice thought, he was certain to stop for coffee.

As the cloud reshaped the sky, light dwindled, and Janice moved out from under the trees. She began asking herself the questions she'd asked her grandmother so many times: Why had the captain left his bride in such a dangerous predicament? And why had she agreed?

Her grandmother never had any answers, and eventually she would grow tired of Janice's questions. "I have the ring," her grandmother would say finally, "and that's the end of that." But Janice never saw the ring; it was hidden in a drawer or locked in a vault—her grandmother was a little vague about it.

But what would the ring prove, Janice wondered now, with

an odd urgency. Would it prove that the girl was a goose, the boy unhinged by panic? She remembered the girl saying—and of course it was the last thing she said, that anybody heard—"You have no reason to be anxious. I am perfectly comfortable alone."

How often Janice had used words to that effect, going by herself to the hospital for an abortion, or to the movies late at night; how often she had polished her independence, setting it up on mantelpieces in countless rented houses.

The sky was darkening. Soon she would have to go inside the tent. The orange juice king had been gone nearly three hours.

Janice went over the old story again. There was something consoling in doing that. She saw, again, the bride's face at the bottom of the shot tower (and surely she had been very pale, with exhilaration or fear), she saw the way she crouched on the ledge above the water. She heard, with the bride's ears, the ladder being drawn up the wall with a harsh, scratching sound, heard the wooden door slam. Did he call, at the bottom, to give her courage, maybe even shout that he loved her?

Probably not, she thought. The captain would not have wanted to attract attention, and besides, he was in a hurry to join his men.

At that moment, Janice thought, the bride's long wait began.

Thunder shouldered up over the mountain. The dark cloud had taken the whole sky. Raindrops fell heavily and widely separated, as though they were being thrown down one by one. Janice crawled into the tent and zipped the flap. It was stuffy, but it felt secure.

At first, she thought, the bride would have been pleasantly excited, reliving the details of the elopement: how she'd risen before dawn, bathed from a china pitcher, and dressed in the blue-ribboned underclothes designed for her trousseau. She might even have tucked up her skirt—voile, lawn, one of those forgotten fabrics—to explore with her finger between her thighs, imagining how he would take her, although girls in those days were not supposed to know. But how could anyone not know, when the body yearned and yearned?

Rain was falling on the taut tent, bouncing off with a ringing sound as she fell asleep.

She woke with a start, feeling cramped. It was dark. The rain continued.

Reaching for her flashlight, she checked her watch. He had been gone six hours.

She began to wonder at what point the bride had realized that her soldier-husband was not coming back: after a day, a week? Would she have survived longer than a week? Probably, since she had water.

Janice turned on her side. Fortunately the tent was water-tight. There was nothing for her to do. It was too dark to read.

Wind was roaring outside. She thought she heard the little stream they'd crossed, combating its banks.

Probably the bride had lain down on the ledge, stretching her legs, pillowing her head on her arms. The stones would have struck cold through her wedding dress.

After a few days, she would have lost track of time, only rousing herself to drink water from her cupped hands. Gradually her hunger would diminish and then cease altogether, to be replaced by a radiant calm. Turning and turning the ring on her finger, the bride must have heard her mother's voice, lamenting, scolding, or a slave humming in the summer kitchen, or the crackle of a wood fire. Gradually those sounds would withdraw, replaced by silence.

During those days, or weeks, did the dying bride count her blessings, knowing now she would never have to endure cracked nipples from nursing, the first tooth at the tender, swollen breast, her husband's diminishing ardor, the demands of running a big house, of being always kind, always capable?

In a way she was lucky, Janice thought, as thunder cracked against the mountain.

She turned on her flashlight to check the time again. He had been gone seven hours.

There was no way to get out to the main road in the darkness and rain, and what would have been the point anyway? The

77

campsite was at least ten miles, maybe further, from the nearest town. Hitchhiking was more dangerous for a woman than staying alone in the dark. In the morning she would walk out.

The morning was ten hours away.

She knew that anything could have happened to him, or nothing. It was impossible to predict another human being's behavior, the mixture of impulse and accident that governed every act.

She set to work to make herself comfortable, taking off her jeans and shoes and letting down her long hair before creeping into her sleeping bag. She was comfortable, but there was no chance of sleep for another two or three hours, no way to press time forward, toward dawn.

The rain continued. Touching the tent, she thought she could feel each drop, shaped by its fall through darkness as the soft lead had been shaped by its fall from the top of the shot tower.

And she went back again, for consolation, to her questions: Why did he leave her there, instead of somewhere safer? Why did she consent to be left?

Then the strange thought—that the bride had chosen to die if he didn't come back—moved again into her mind.

How could a girl of eighteen or nineteen make such a decision? How could she know what she would miss?

No, Janice thought, the bride wanted to live. As long as she

78

had the strength, she shouted and shouted; she scrabbled at the wall until her fingers bled. She wanted life, with or without the captain, her life, whatever it might be.

Janice zipped the sleeping bag up to her chin. She did not check her watch. The night, she knew, was pacing over her.

The rain stopped at last and it grew cold; she shivered inside the bag.

A thin moon sailed out from behind the departing clouds. Unzipping the tent opening, Janice saw the inky shadows of the pines across the meadow. The drenched grass was silver. And she knew, without any doubt, the girl had chosen life. The girl would always choose life.

A GIFT FOR BURNING

Of course it's the boy. Why else?

Yes, I know he's a grown man now, on the verge of middle age, and I admire what he's done, of course I do. What mother wouldn't?

But as for claiming responsibility, or believing I influenced him: No. I made more mistakes with him than I've ever been able to forgive myself for, even after all these years: the bad marriages, four of them (not that they were all bad, but it's the bad parts I remember), the worse divorces, when I fought for things that didn't matter—only that never occurred to me till years later. And all the time here was this small child, this boy, sprung from some forgotten hope (or delusion), sailing his paper boats in the creek in Ohio, digging to China in the sand on that island off the South Carolina coast (that was the fisherman stepdad), or wandering around in the Metropolitan Museum when he was supposed to be in school (that was the big-time city councilperson). And all the time—or most of it—I was too distracted by my own heart to pay much attention to him.

Yes, of course I did the usual things: put breakfast on the table in front of him (and he was picky, wouldn't eat anything but real sure-enough hot oatmeal with honey), tried to see he was dressed for school on time—and those schools! I never realized until years later when he wrote his first book how he hated them—the deadly progressive schools alternating with total chaos of the public kind; yes, I can assure you, that came as an eye-opener to me, and I've spent a good deal of time on my knees praying whoever it is for forgiveness.

Did that first book make me angry?

No. Nothing can make me angry now.

It was only a novel, after all—I used to remind so-called friends of that—and it was well-written. He has a sense of words, the boy—the young man, the nearly middle-aged man— and I appreciate that. Where'd he get it? Who knows. He was always a big reader. I don't question where gifts come from; it's enough just to enjoy them.

And that book did reveal to me what he'd gone through as a teenager, when after two failures I thought I'd found him a real father, at last. The city councilperson did have a feel for kids, but the trouble was he also had a feel for power, and it's a hell of a lot more exciting to do battle with New York City politicos than to sit at home supervising a talk-back stepson's homework. So what was good in theory didn't work at all, or at least that's what I thought; the boy let me know different in that sequence of sonnets he published in that little mag; did you see them? Dedicated to his second stepfather, can you believe it—of course you can. You weren't around—weren't hatched yet—during those awful years.

Yes, awful.

I don't mince words, wouldn't if he was here himself. (No, he doesn't visit very often, he's made a life for himself in the North, that's where his work and his reputation are, and here I am, stranded at the tip of Florida in this sandy little resort; why would he want to come here? Why do I stay here? That's another question altogether, my Dear.)

Yes, look at your notes, I'm sure we haven't begun to cover the questions you planned on the plane. I know how you interviewers are—you aren't the first, his Pulitzer brought you in swarms. You claim to have an open mind, but the way you shape your questions always reveals you've already decided who I am: Good Mother, Bad Mother—is there really much difference?

Sorry.

It's been years since I was defined in terms of my role as the boy's mother. Let alone the young man's mother. I came down

83

here, as silly as it sounds, to sit under the palm trees on that long line of beach you see from the window and write poetry, and I've done that—not that you've read any of it, I almost never send it out, and when I do, it comes flying back: not in the style of the times, and so forth. But I think of myself, I really do, as a poet, and then you come down here and try to drag me back into that other definition . . .

No. I'm not jealous of the boy's success. Everything has its price, and when I was his age, I was spending nearly all my time and energy getting married and unmarried and married again. He won't do that, the boy. I doubt he'll ever get married at all, although he always has some bright young woman to take care of things—you've met the latest, haven't you—Veronica? I like her, by the way, and I've managed to bite my tongue when I'm tempted to ask her what she gets out of it.

No, none of my husbands performed that role—what a choice of words! You sound like we hire lovers for the services they provide. That wouldn't be such a bad idea, except in those days— the fifties, when I was doing all the marrying and unmarrying— there weren't any men available to serve. They weren't interested in being muses, either, in fact it just wouldn't have been possible to discuss it. What did service or being a muse have to do with true love, anyway? And we all wanted true love, yes indeed we did, back then. Remember, we were coming out of the forties when all the women went home and the suburbs started to grow into preserves to keep us safe and sound.

Did I tell you how the boy decorated that basement "Family Room" (I can't help it, I have to put it in quotes) when he was nine or so?

Farm animals, no less, and the fisherman—who was in the driver's seat, that year—made him paint them out; I sat on the steps and watched the boy destroy his work—his masterpieces— with tears running down his face and tears running down mine. But what could tears do, I ask you? I never stopped that man, not once, and there were other things he did.

No, I'm not going to discuss that. Water over the dam. Besides, you should know, Young Lady, artists aren't made the easy way. It's not hot chocolate and oatmeal cookies for them. It's the tough way, the long way, the solitary way. I may be a hidden poet of limited talent but this much I know: the tough way I unintentionally provided for myself and for the boy—the young man, excuse me—may have been the best launch of his talent.

Sorry. I don't mean to step on your toes. I know the theory as well as you do: talent gets nurtured (what a horrible word that is, I do hope you'll put it in quotes, too) only by some loving mama sitting by the stove with a plateful of something delicious and just the right kind of vanilla-flavored praise and acceptance.

Well, that's just a crock of _____, believe me. If I'd been

an easier person, a better mother, whatever, you wouldn't have taken that long flight from New York to interview me. And the boy wouldn't be up in Washington accepting his Pulitzer for what is, after all, only his third book; he'd be some nice accountant or dentist, talking to his clients about how he once had this dream.

No, I'm not talking child abuse, I'm talking about the sorrows of life and how early they begin and how soon they are accepted: that's what makes an artist—too lonely a road for me to travel when I was young. But the boy—the young man—seems to have set his feet on it, although as Napoleon's mother is supposed to have said, *Pourvue que ça dur*. No, I won't translate, that's what dictionaries are for.

Yes, he did come down here once, it was two or three years ago, I think, I don't keep track of time. I was house-proud and wanted him to see the first place I'd bought with my own money and set up to live in alone. By then the fourth husband had gone off and I was determined to be on my own.

He came down, it was Easter, I think, and we spent a couple of days trying to make up for lost time, which can't be done, but there's no harm in trying. He had his little laptop machine and he used to sit on the porch all morning with his cup of coffee getting cold on the rail; I'd look out every now and then and see him watching that palm tree rustle or pinning his eyes on the far line of the sea. I don't know what he was working on, it didn't seem appropriate to ask. Yes, I suppose it could have been this last book, the one that got him the praise: his novel about the end of the world.

Let me go on, please—it's a pleasure to remember, I don't do it that much.

Around noon I asked him if he wanted to go to the beach— speaking softly through the screen door, I still thought inspiration was a butterfly you could brush off with a sound. He got up, closed that little machine (I don't believe in them. I write my first drafts in long hand and little Elissa down the block types them up for me on her computer), and went to get his bathing suit. I packed a couple of sandwiches and a thermos of something cool and we took the two bikes—you saw them downstairs, the pink and the aquamarine, I keep them in the front hall now, there's been a lot of thievery around here lately—and we pedaled in a leisurely sort of way down to the beach, left the bikes in the shade—we didn't even lock them, as I remember—and carried the towels and the picnic out to the beach.

This place wasn't as crowded then, and we found a cove where we could spread out our things. Both of us were cautious about the sun but we love the warmth, and stretching out on towels and listening to the waves breaking a few feet away—well, I don't think there's anything better.

Sure, I still go there, just about every day, in fact, if we get this over with soon enough, I plan to take my lunch.

Yes, we were trying to make up for lost time, and no, it can't be done, but we did tell each other some of our various versions of that crazy life we'd shared.

Like the last time I got unmarried: the boy was old enough by then to be fully aware of all the arguments and the late-night calls to lawyers and the rest of the predictable frenzy; he asked to come to court and I let him do it though it meant cutting school—they wouldn't give him an excuse, told me the whole idea was inappropriate. Well, no surprise, you know how they are about real life, they think the whole thing is inappropriate.

So there he was, sitting or rather slouching in court every day. It was the time when he had three earrings in one ear and a big blond ruff sticking up out of the top of his head; and I'm sure that nice Southern judge thought he was looking at the evil fruit of our preposterous union—it was with the carpenter, and he was one of my strong points. He'd never done a damn thing for the boy although the main reason I married him, I have to admit, aside from the fact that he was good-looking and an ace in bed (rarer than you might expect), was that he purported to be good daddy material, had raised five children of his own just about single-handed, but it turned out that did it for him, his daddy material was exhausted, he just wanted to drink beer and loaf, which was when the boy got started on liquor, and it did him a lot more harm, if you ask me, than the illegal stuff.

No, this is not confidential. He talks about it in this new book, shows how it'll bring about the end of the world. I'm not telling any secrets out of school.

Anyway, we were in court fighting over money, the carpenter and I, and there are always observers in court. You never know who you may see sitting in those wooden pews; it's a public event, the way hangings were: free excitement, a spectator sport, especially when there's a fair amount of money involved.

Of course you know that, the boy couldn't afford to be a writer otherwise. I assumed—

Well, if he's never discussed it, that's his right, but since it's my money, I'll talk about it all I want. As far as I'm concerned, the only justification for inherited money is that it makes artists and social activists.

No, I don't want to talk about where the money came from, that's a different conversation altogether and you've already taken up a lot of my time. I told you I want to get to the beach.

But let me finish about court. I know this isn't one of the questions on that yellow pad, but so what? You're in my house, and I have a right to talk about what I think is important.

All right. Truce, then.

As I was saying, the boy was lounging in court every day, and sometimes at the break I'd see him talking to a couple of black men in turned-around collars who were there for some reason or other. I didn't know them, and I don't think the boy knew them, either, but since I'd raised him to be color-blind—that was one of my big missions, as a mom—he didn't see any reason to avoid them. I thought they were there to wish me well; in fact, one of them sent me a teddy bear, can you believe it, by the court reporter, on a day when the carpenter was digging into some pretty dirty stuff about my behavior. I'm no angel, I can tell you that, but it's a different matter when someone with the will to harm brings it out in court . . .

I have to admit I carried that teddy bear to court every day, and the first faces I'd see when we came in—my attorneys and me, they used to flank me like a battalion—were those two black preachers smiling and nodding at me, and my boy there beside them. He started sitting in the pew with them the second day, I think.

Well, they are like pews.

Anyway, I was glad to have the support of those men; I've always believed solidarity between women and black people would bring about the changes we want—think of the power of that block, but we haven't been able to put it together; we think we have to make a hierarchy out of oppression, decide which one has it worst, and so on, and then divide along those lines. A terrible mistake.

A Gift for Burning

The boy and me and those two black preachers—that's where the power lay, in that courtroom, not with the judge or the carpenter and his pals and attorneys. The disadvantaged, whether through youth, gender or race, pack a punch that outdoes education and sophistication and even money; we connect with them on a visceral level because everyone at some time or another has felt disadvantaged or at least left out. Even me.

On the last day, after I'd won—you can call it that, if you want—I was going down the escalator with the boy. We were both too tired to smile much; I was already beginning to figure how much that particular victory was going to cost me, and I don't mean in money alone. There's scorched earth, emotionally—

Well, anyway, there we were with the fruits of our success, so to speak, and I still had that ridiculous teddy bear in my arms, and who should be at the foot of the escalator—and I don't know how they got down there so fast—but *our* two black preachers, beaming.

They reached out to help me off the escalator, and oh it felt good, those two solid handsome men letting me know that we had something in common, my humiliation and despair there in the courtroom was something like what they'd felt as black men walking the streets of that godforsaken Southern town. Because they knew the win was not a win really, just another sort of devastation.

Red Car

Maybe you can't believe that, looking at me—I always wear silk in the tropics—and this beautiful house and of course Amelia letting you in the front door. No use to say to you that money isn't everything; I'll let the boy do that, in due time.

What did the preachers want?

Nothing much, really.

Just for us to ride down to the neighborhood center they were running in the ghetto. I was dead-beat but the boy was determined to go—I hadn't a clue why, then—and because I was so grateful for their support, I let myself be drawn along into the powerful car which the bigger one of the two was driving, and it didn't even occur to me to wonder how that car had been paid for—we were at the sunken end of the economy, the late eighties; I just sank back in those leather seats and hugged my teddy bear and felt the air-conditioning and said to myself over and over again, *Never again, Never again*—about court, and marrying and unmarrying.

We got down into the ghetto, and it's a fierce experience, the ghetto, wherever it happens, and it happens everywhere; have you seen the streets behind the wharves here? You really should before you get on the plane, there won't be any artists coming out of those houses, you can count on that.

No, I'm not bitter, and I know we need social services. The society's so unjust that anything we can do, publicly or privately, is just a way of recognizing that injustice, of institutionalizing it, really: "Let them eat cake."

That's what the two reverends were doing with their neighborhood center—teaching boys how to improve their basketball skills, offering cooking classes for the girls; poverty reinforces stereotypes, have you noticed? They were building up another generation of dependent people—the reverends wanted them to be dependent, because whoever controls the handouts controls the future. They were the conduit for a fair amount of state and federal monies that were coming into the ghetto to cure unemployment and drug use blab blab blah, and of course they were also exploiting the causes of drug use and unemployment because once you control one end of the cycle you control the other end too. Know what I mean? I guess not. Well, maybe you will someday, if you get out of New York.

Anyway, the boy was impressed by what he saw—I was too tired and disoriented to notice much of anything—and a few days later, when the bigger of the two reverends paid me an unsolicited call, the boy, who was at home (he'd been suspended from school for something or other, maybe it was the time he'd spent in court), came running down the stairs—he'd seen that big car from his window—and insisted I had to write out a sizable check for the reverend's do-good project—even had the gall to remind me how I'd hung onto the teddy bear during the trial. So I did.

Red Car

Write out the check, of course.

I don't remember for how much. It doesn't matter, really, it was a pay-off and nobody with any sense counts dollars and cents when it's a question of a pay-off. I was grateful, and the boy was grateful, and that was all that mattered at the time.

No, I didn't ask anyone for advice, it didn't occur to me. I was isolated, if you will—all women going through battles are isolated, it's a given. Don't you know that Adrienne Rich poem about loneliness? Well, go home and look it up. There's no courage without loneliness, my Dear.

So the check was written, accepted with thanks, and endorsed to somebody else—I remember noticing that later when I went over my canceled checks. Eventually I found out who that other person was, but that's another story.

I thought that chapter of my life was closed—and I was eager to close it, you can understand that—but as it turned out the reverends found a foothold in my life, or rather, in my son's.

He was going into his darkest time, the time his third book describes, with some artistic leeway, of course—he has a splendid imagination.

I thought he was sinking—I didn't know for sure. All I did know was that he was sleeping all day, never went back to school—not a great loss, I thought at the time—but he wasn't reading or playing the piano or riding his bike, either. His life had drawn in, just the way mine had——I was persona non grata in that community, they don't like outspoken women who win——who does? I'm not even sure I like them myself.

So the boy was lying in bed upstairs till four or five every day and then the phone would start to ring, and when I'd answer it, there'd be these blurred nameless voices on the other end——I never knew who they were, not his old friends from school, that's for sure——and I'd holler up the stairs and he'd come and stick his face over the banister——and what a face! Everything was written there——and then if he felt like it, and he usually did, he'd pick up the extension, and I'd hear a lot of "Hey, man" and "What's up, man?" and "Nothing much"——there never is much up in those lives at four o'clock in the afternoon.

And in fifteen minutes he'd be out of there——

No, I don't know how this connects to his success and his talent and I don't care much either, I'm telling you a story, have the courtesy not to interrupt.

Very well. Now, where was I?

Oh yes——he'd be up and out of there, no food all day, nothing——and when I looked at him, I saw he was dwindling down to skin and bones, and those blue eyes shining, shining.

I thought I was losing him.

I thought he was losing himself.

So when the handsome young black man moved in with us, I

was grateful. He was soft-spoken, well-spoken—some woman had done her work. He maybe had no education but he sounded beautiful; and he was beautiful, tall and athletic, and when he had on my son's clothes, which was what he wore mostly, he was a sight to be seen—and I thought he'd drive the boy home from those parties and make sure he wasn't killed in an accident. At least that was our agreement, his and mine. And the boy didn't get killed in an accident, although I guess that didn't have much to do with the handsome young black man. He was the big reverend's nephew, it seemed.

He moved in with us, and every now and then they'd honor me with their presence at a meal, and we'd talk about poetry and beauty and light—the three of us high as kites off grandiosity, the most illegal of all illegal drugs: two young males who thought they had the world by the tail, for reasons I wasn't aware of, and one middle-aged woman suffering from the same delusion. And of course I paid for our guest's college tuition—he was clearly going places, a candidate for tokenism if I ever saw one—and I gave them both cash when they needed it for all kinds of purposes: car repair, new clothes, meals out—not a huge amount of cash, no, but enough to fuel some of those episodes you've been raving about in his latest book.

What did that *New York Times* reviewer call it? An Orwellian descent into the depths?

A Gift for Burning

Oh yes.

Well, that went on for a while, maybe three months, and meantime my son was fading away in front of me, just dwindling down to bone, and I was drinking and smoking and listening to country music and trying to believe we were all flying high together in our dream-making machine. Sometimes during those nights I thought we were even dreaming in tandem, me and the handsome young black man and the dwindling-away boy...

Yes, it came to an end. Of course it came to an end, or you wouldn't be sitting here today.

The reverends hadn't shown up in a while although our guest often told me they sent their regards and so forth and I knew it was only a question of time before that big car turned up in my driveway and they would need another check for the good work they were doing in the ghetto, but I didn't allow myself to worry about that—one day at a time, you know.

Then one winter Sunday morning—I'd woken up without a hangover for once and was actually considering going to church—the handsome young black man who'd been out all night with the boy came in with a baby.

Yes.

A baby about two months old, I'd say, and white.

Yes. A boy.

And white.

Red Car

My son was in the kitchen fixing himself coffee and the handsome young black man, our guest, came into my bedroom where I was trying to decide what would be appropriate for a sinner to wear to church—bright red, maybe?—and he had in his arms this adorable infant, sound asleep.

He said it was his.

I couldn't very well ask him why he had a white baby, for all I knew, the baby's mother was white. It wasn't the sort of question I could allow myself to ask.

He put that baby in my arms, and I went all soft the way we do with babies—and he asked me if I'd watch little Benny for a few hours while he and the boy slept off whatever they'd been into the night before; and when I felt that baby's warm sweet weight in my arms, by God, I almost said yes.

It was that close.

And then through some grace I looked at that handsome young man's face, and I saw his smile and I knew there was something wrong with that smile. It was just too sweet. He had made me a Madonna or something like that, his smile said, and there wasn't any need for church or anything else; I could just sit there in my stained old bathrobe and hold his son—if it was his son—and be happy and mild and smooth for hours and hours while he and the boy slept the sleep of the nearly dead.

My God. I almost did it. I really did.

Somehow I managed to push that baby back into the young man's arms. I'll never know where I found the strength because of course I love to be needed and all the rest of it.

The baby almost fell on the floor between us because our guest wasn't prepared to take him back, and his smile ended fast and he said something I didn't quite catch—didn't want to catch—and it was the first time I saw his surface crack and I asked him out of nowhere if my son had told him how I'd always wanted more than one baby of my own.

He said my son had never discussed such a thing with him but he knew all women loved babies and besides I was so lonely.

I am not lonely, I said, and that Adrienne Rich poem came to my aid, and I said, *I'm a rowboat that knows it's not the winter light or the mud but wood with a gift for burning.*

So you see poetry saved my life.

Yes, it did.

I know you think I'm being melodramatic and maybe in a way I am, but without that line of hers coming to mind— muddled no doubt but still powerful—I'd be in that old farmhouse still with the baby a teenager and my life redefined according to someone else's dream.

I'd already done that four times.

Red Car

Sure, it was the turning point and if you doubt me, go to page 397 in my son's latest and you'll see the way he described it. It was a turning point for him, too, though in a different way.

No, I don't know what happened to that baby. And frankly I refuse to think about it.

It took another arrest after a party that left my house in a shambles, but a week later the boy and the handsome young man had both packed some of their clothes and some of my possessions—all my good jewelry and most of the silver, wedding present stuff, I wasn't sorry to see it go—and hightailed it out of there. And I didn't hear from my son for more than a year.

I don't know where he was. Down in the ghetto, probably, with the reverends and their nephew, if he was their nephew. Eventually he spent some time in jail—he says now they set him up, but of course he was in the wrong place at the wrong time— and then he went into rehab for a while, paid for it himself, I insisted on that, and got into AA and started smoking and drinking coffee instead of the other stuff; and a few years back he adopted a young black boy—no, I don't believe it could have been that baby, life isn't that neat—and began writing and you know what came next.

Success.

It's his, my Dear, I don't claim any part in it.

All right, I will accept some responsibility for putting that baby back in our guest's arms.

Because it's true nobody becomes an artist or anything else worthwhile until she or he puts off the easy stuff.

Good weather. Food. Excitement. Love. It varies from person to person. Whatever your easy answer is.

PORN

The talk could only have taken place in the car, where they did not have to look at each other. Arthur kept his eyes locked on the road and Margaret, out of habit, locked her eyes on the road along with his. Now and then she glanced at him, but Arthur's face in profile was always a little bewildering and so she turned back to the road.

"Are you bored with me?" she asked after a while—the obvious question, but she felt it needed to be asked.

"What's that got to do with renting a video?"

"Then you are bored with me."

"No."

His tone was not convincing. She thought for a moment, organizing herself. Younger, she would have reacted with a bark of laughter or a cry of pain; now, in her stable fifties, she had learned to wait for her more modulated reaction. "I tried wearing a garter belt for you last summer, but it didn't work at all."

His hand crawled toward hers on the seat and clasped her fingers comfortably. "This is not about you, or me," he said in his calm doctor's voice. "It's just something I thought we might enjoy."

"But wouldn't it lead to other things?" Margaret asked apprehensively.

"What other things?" Arthur's profile was smiling.

Margaret equivocated. She did not like the uneasy and distrustful part of her character that Arthur's rare forays into strangeness aroused. "Perhaps they don't have VCRs at the inn."

"I asked when I made the reservation. They do."

A memory from ten years earlier came to her rescue. "Aren't they always sort of violent?"

"I won't rent that kind," he said.

"I remember reading somewhere they actually kill the women."

"That's not the kind I like."

She registered this slowly. "So you've looked at them before?"

"When I was married." He rarely shed a light on that state, or condition; Margaret, who'd been married twice, could not imagine how Arthur, who didn't know how to boil an egg or do his own laundry, could have withstood the fearsome demands of matrimony. Shared work, she'd learned both times, took more time than work done alone, and was never entirely satisfactory.

"Did the videos help?" she asked.

"Not much. Ann would look for a while, but then she'd turn over and go to sleep." And he told a joke about marriage being the best way to douse a woman's sexual urge.

"I don't like that joke," Margaret said, looking out the window. They were driving on the old turnpike that wound its way upstate. In the swamp she could see from the car window, skunk cabbage was pushing up its pointed leaves.

"You must have heard it too often," Arthur said, moving his big hand back to the steering wheel. In the course of his practice in one of the prosperous suburbs, he drove many miles a day, linking clinic and hospital and office with long loops; he seemed, Margaret often thought, to be a part of his car, sitting well down in the sunken seat with his right knee slightly elevated to balance his foot on the accelerator. Even without his seat belt—and he always wore his seat belt—he looked glued.

"Perhaps we might try it, then," Margaret said, remembering with a little unhappy vagueness that going to bed with Arthur was no longer delightful or surprising but a Saturday night ritual of surprising vacuity. Since they had known each other almost a year, she had resigned herself to the falling of their emotional temperature, which seemed to decline at the same rate toward a cool forty-two degrees. It had been this way during both her marriages and all her affairs; the heat had finally failed. Now she wondered if there might be a way, an artificial way, even, to restore the gleam to Arthur's eyes and the eager reach to his hands.

"Will it make you uncomfortable?" he asked.

Challenged, she said stoutly that she was looking forward to the experience. They drove the rest of the way in contented silence.

The country inn was about what they expected, pretty and prim, with the remoteness from its original function as a marginal farm that reassured people visiting from the city. No henhouses or pigsties remained to offend with unfamiliar sounds and odors, and the outdoor privy had been transformed into a sort of hermit's retreat with a rocking chair set before a scenic view.

Nothing, in short, was available to distract them from the prospect of a long evening alone—it was barely five o'clock, they had left the city early—and the dining room promised to hold them for an hour at most over a supper of baked fish and potatoes and suspiciously green broccoli. Arthur had a glass of wine but Margaret refrained; she was already a little sleepy, and she wanted to be wide awake for the viewing—as she thought of it.

After coffee, Arthur volunteered to go alone into the village to rent the video, and Margaret was relieved; she imagined the side aisles where that sort of thing might be displayed, usually with a warning sign about children. She couldn't imagine herself in her gray tweed trousers and blazer and Arthur in his corduroys and nice old sweater peering, together, at the display, comparing this one and that.

While he was gone, she took a quick shower, brushed her thin brown hair, and put on the satin nightgown, a real extravagance, which she saved for these weekends, washing it out by hand and ironing it with a cool iron between times. She never wore that nightgown when she was alone as, she realized, she never assumed the gallant poses or expressed the delight and enthusiasm that used to come almost naturally when she was in bed with Arthur. Alone, she set the alarm, aimed the bedside light carefully, and sank with a kind of ecstasy into her current book; nothing, she had realized several times in the past months, felt so good, so profoundly relaxing and rejuvenating, as going to bed alone.

She did not want the relationship to end; ends of all kinds were difficult for her, and she often felt helpless and dejected in the aftermath. There was always the possibility, too, that this was her last—that there would be no other. Perhaps it is time for porn, she thought uneasily.

She climbed up onto the high old bed. The sheets were chilly. As she pulled the faded rose-colored comforter up under her chin, she noticed with satisfaction that it was silk, and then tried to imagine its history. It smelled of mothballs; she marveled as she lay there that moths still existed in the civilized world, along with all the devices used to discourage them, and remembered the smell of the cedar closet where her mother had stored their winter woolens. The massed shoulders of suits, hanging there, were her only memory of her father, who had left them early, taking only one change of clothes, as her mother often remarked, in a small canvas bag.

And was never heard from again, she thought, adjusting the big flat pillows under her head; that was the way it used to be. When a man decided that marriage was no longer what he wanted, he lit out for the territory, leaving wife and children to fend for themselves, which was perhaps a better way to go about it, Margaret thought. Several of her women friends had delinquent husbands, divorced or not, who reappeared at awkward intervals, scooping up children who had finally become accustomed to their absence, visiting the saga of their misadventures on their exhausted wives. Margaret imagined how those children, later, would imagine those fathers—as heroes, or at least adventurers. She had, she felt, a more realistic version of her father, as a man who simply couldn't stick, a man who had to go away.

She sat up and pushed back the rose-colored comforter.

Arthur had been gone far too long; the village was only a mile or so away. She reached for her purse to count her money and check her credit cards; it would be terrible to be left with no way to pay the bill. At that moment, he walked in the door and asked her what she was doing, diving into her purse.

PORN

She didn't need to tell him. The plastic case in his hand seemed to take up all the space between them. "They're on DVD now," he said.

"That's progress, I guess," she said.

Arthur didn't laugh. He was far too intent on getting the disc into the player, which took some doing; the buttons were small, and their labels were hard to read. Margaret suggested his glasses, but Arthur—as though offended by the suggestion—got down on his hands and knees to study the buttons at close quarters, and eventually found the right combination.

A mass of music erupted from the blank screen, and Margaret shrank back against the headboard; she had expected a volley of words, perhaps, artificial dialogue to cover the actions portrayed, but not the unwelcome romance of a full score.

"The people who make these things must think we're fools," she said.

Arthur sat back on his heels to look at the first images, and stayed in that position for a full five minutes. Margaret realized she had never seen him keep such an uncomfortable posture for so long.

She tried to concentrate on the screen rather than on the top of his head, where his gray hair grew in patchy abundance. She found herself intrigued by the back of his neck: a long, sinewy dent disappeared into his collar. She tried to remember whether the dent went down between his shoulder blades. Suddenly, Arthur seemed fragile, crouching there, and she felt guilty as though her eyes were blows aimed at that pale groove on the back of his neck—and it was true she had been thinking disloyal thoughts, lately. The blind stubbornness that had thrust her out of other unsatisfactory relationships came to her aid, and she summoned him peremptorily to sit on the bed beside her.

Arthur was still watching with a silent absorption that frightened Margaret, who imagined this was the way he stared at slides of suspicious cells, or perhaps even at the bodies of his patients. She knew from his accounts that certain of these women aroused his sexual interest, and now and then he found a book that excited him, as well—often one from the old, outlawed repertoire, now so completely forgotten: *Lady Chatterley's Lover*, or *Tropic of Capricorn*—books their parents might have smuggled back from summer trips to Europe. In general, she thought, Arthur's approach to life was light and wavering, and she was more comfortable with that than with his fixed stare at the screen.

"Look," he said, tapping her arm, and she was reminded of one of her sixth-grade students who tried insistently to get her attention with scowls or grasping motions at the air—a stupid boy whose papers were an agony to read.

"I don't want to look," she said mulishly, and was tempted to hide her head under the rose-colored comforter.

PORN

The images were everywhere now, released into the air.

Arthur didn't seem to hear. He was leaning forward so intently her eyes followed his as they had on the road, and she saw images she at first took for advertisements: shaving devices promoted with smooth thighs, hairless torsos. Then she deciphered the ancient choreography of bodies and felt a flash, as though she had received a recognizable signal through a set of receptors she hadn't been aware of; I speak this language, she thought, amazed.

Now, she realized, a beautiful woman was spread like a filleted fish on a bed of ice; she seemed stupefied, her fixed eyes glaring. Her thighs gripped the head of a young man whose hands held her large breasts securely yet nonchalantly, like handlebars. When another young man appeared, penis at the ready, and inserted it like a thermometer in the spread woman's mouth, Margaret protected her own mouth with her hand. She did not feel that the woman was willing, or unwilling; she seemed to have suspended her animation, hanging in the void the two men had created.

Arthur seized her hand and placed it on his groin.

"What are they doing to that woman?" Margaret gasped.

"Pleasuring her," Arthur said, thickly. She had never imagined him using such an expression.

"That would not pleasure me," she announced, taking her hand away. She was sick with misery now; she had seen the woman's face, and it seemed familiar, like one of the women she had lunch with, or even one of her neighbors. It was not the face itself, she realized, but its suspended expression that was familiar; the woman was out of her mind.

She kept her hands over her eyes, after that.

When the show was finished, Arthur carefully ejected the disc and returned it to its case, which he placed on the table next to the door so he would not forget to return it in the morning.

Meanwhile Margaret was noticing details of the room she did not particularly want to commit to memory: the cloudlike bursts of roses on the wallpaper, the awful green slipper chair, the grimy fireplace, the rocking chair beside it no one rocked in. The room was empty; it was filled, regularly, yet it remained empty, a pantomime of a room. She turned her head and saw the two foil-wrapped chocolates and the breakfast menu on the bedside table, and realized these, too, were symbols of something that never happened—comfort, intimacy, satisfaction.

Arthur picked up the menu and began to consider the choices. "Why didn't you want to look?" he asked.

"I expected it to be different."

"How?"

"I used to think it would be better, somehow," she said, by way of answer.

He laughed, and marked an item on the menu with the tiny pencil provided. She knew he would hang the card on the outside knob of their door, as advised, and that at some time in the night, sleepless, she would hear the scurry of feet as the card was surreptitiously removed, and then there would be a banging on the door at whatever hour Arthur had chosen for their breakfast, and this would wake her from her first sleep—and all of this had happened before, and would always be entirely acceptable.

After he undressed, Arthur rolled into bed and took her in his arms. To their shared amazement, Margaret found herself responding. She bit into his neck; she was so intent she hardly noticed when he shrieked, and she did not apologize, as she would doubtless do in the morning.

His Sons

"It's time," Tom told me one day.

"Yes?"

"I want you to meet my boys. We'll go to the country."

That Friday he bundled me into his car and we swooped across town to the apartment building where his two sons lived with their mother.

"I'll come up with you," I said, unfastening my seat belt, but he had already disappeared into the lobby.

I reached for the box of chocolates I'd brought the boys and the novel I hoped to finish reading during the weekend.

In a while Tom came out with a son on either side. I was surprised to see that the eldest reached almost to his father's shoulder. I had imagined them still small, although I knew their ages.

Tom directed both boys into the back seat, and then leaned

through the window to introduce me. "Caroline, this is Lenny. This is David."

I looked at their faces which seemed childlike now that their bodies were folded out of sight. "I've been wanting to meet you," I said.

Lenny, the eldest, looked at me.

David said, "Oh yeah?" He was ten years old, heavier than his brother. He kept glancing at me as his father started the car. Finally, he said, "I thought you had blond hair."

"Are you disappointed?"

"Mom found blond hairs on Daddy's jacket once."

"Is your mother blond?"

"She dyes her hair. I don't know what color it is."

"Brown," Tom said.

"You shouldn't just tell anyone she dyes her hair," Lenny said.

"I'm not just anyone," I told him, watching Tom wrestling the car into the traffic on Riverside Drive.

"How long will it take us to get there?" David asked presently.

"The same amount of time it takes when you go with your mother," Tom told him.

"I remember once you drove ninety miles an hour," David said.

"I haven't driven that fast since you were born. Now stop complaining."

"I'm not complaining, I'm hungry."

I passed the box of chocolates over the seat. David squealed.

"What did you give them?" Tom asked.

"Chocolates. Would you like some?"

He declined with a brusqueness that startled me.

The boys began to divide up the candy, squabbling at first and then working out a trading system.

"David's teeth are full of holes," Tom muttered.

"Next time I'll bring the sugarless kind."

"The dentist's bill last month was over a thousand dollars. His mother can't get him to brush." Then suddenly, to David: "Listen, you can have one more piece, and that's it. Give the candy back to Caroline."

"Oh, Daddy! I only had two cavities, last time, little ones."

Lenny said, "And did he throw a fit. They had to give him enough novocain to kill a pig."

"I did not throw a fit. My pain threshold is low."

"That's enough," Tom said.

It was not long before David began again. "Who was that black lady, Daddy, that drove up with us one time?"

"She wasn't black, she was Korean," Tom said, "and that was a long time ago."

"She was nice. I liked her! She sent me a big box of fudge for my birthday. Why don't you bring her to the country anymore?"

Tom answered evenly, "Because she decided she wanted to get married, and I told her I'm not the man for that."

"Why not, Pop?" Lenny's voice was careless.

"I'll tell you some day."

"I think you could explain right now," David said.

"No."

"Well, I think you could."

"Damn it," Tom said, under his breath.

"I heard you! I heard you!"

Tom pulled over to the side of the road, and then turned and slapped David's cheek. It sounded like a board hitting a pumpkin.

Then he turned the car back onto the throughway and Lenny began to talk, weaving his words through his brother's sobs. "Pop, I'm going to be in the class play this year."

"What part?"

"Here," I said, handing David a tissue.

"It's *Julius Caesar* and I play a soldier."

"I'll come see you," Tom promised. Then he went on listening to Lenny for a while.

"Are you all right?" he asked me, a little later.

"I suppose so."

"I'm sorry," he said carefully. "Sometimes I lose control."

Thinking of the implications, I began to wonder why I'd had

such high hopes of Tom, and then I remembered the story of the Bishop of India.

"Would you like to hear how your father and I met?" I asked, and David's sobs began to run down. "It was a big party. Your father and I didn't know anyone there."

"I knew Carter Jones and his wife," Tom said.

"I didn't know anyone there. I almost didn't go because I was afraid I'd stand in a corner the whole time, never get up the courage to introduce myself. Thank God I did—get up the courage, I mean—because the second man I met was your father."

"Who was the first?" David asked.

"That's another story. Anyway, we started talking, and it turned out we had all kinds of things in common. I don't mean cities and colleges, I mean quirks in our lives. I lost my father when I was five, and Tom as you know lost his when he was three."

I realized from their expressions that they did not know. "I was brought up on my grandmother's tales about Ireland, and your father was raised by his grandmother who knew lots of stories, too." Again, they looked blank.

I went on, "My grandmother used to tell me about her uncle who was the Bishop of India. He complained that the monkeys made fun of him outside his window when he said his prayers at night. When I told your father that story, he said his great-uncle had been in India with the British Army, and suddenly we both knew those two gentlemen had been acquainted, maybe even friends."

David said, "I don't get it."

Tom explained, "Caroline is an incurable romantic. She thinks we were brought together by fate."

"You make it sound like a disease," I said.

"Another time. . . . What are we going to eat, boys, when we get to the country? Did you remember to check in the freezer last weekend?"

"I looked," Lenny said, "and there's a whole lot of sherbet with ice on the top, and there's French fries, lots of packages."

"That won't make a meal," Tom said.

"And there's a duck or a goose or maybe it's a chicken."

Tom turned off the throughway. "We'll put that fowl in the oven and heat the French fries to go with it and have the sherbet for dessert. How does that sound?"

I laughed at his chop-licking appetite and reminded him that a frozen bird would take hours to cook.

"We have plenty of time," Tom said.

Actually it was a Rock Cornish hen. Tom took it out of the freezer as soon as we walked in the house. "Pretty small," he said. I thought it was a bad omen that we were going to have to satisfy ourselves with a bird hardly bigger than my hand.

I lit the oven, and then looked inside a cabinet for a roasting pan.

"Take off your coat," Tom told me. "You haven't even looked around the house."

"I don't need to. There's a rack in the hall with jackets and rubber boots, and fishing rods behind the bathroom door, and in the attic there are old magazines and rat poison."

Tom smiled and turned away. "David!" he shouted over the thump of music from the living room. "Come in here and set the table!"

David came through the door slowly. His dangling hand brushed Tom's whisky glass off the kitchen table. Tom stood over him while he picked up the fragments. "It's Lenny's turn to set the table," David said, sniffling a little. "I did it last time."

To my surprise, Tom relented. Lenny slipped in and began to lay out knives and forks.

I put the frozen bird in the oven and looked around the kitchen. A row of dulled equipment stood against an olive-painted wall, and the calendar from the local hardware store hung cockeyed next to a bleary sink. "Two years old," I said to no one in particular. Tom had gone off.

David explained, "Mom says a kitchen is supposed to be ugly."

"She never said that." Lenny placed the last glass and retreated into the living room.

"Do you like it here?" I asked David, who was still dawdling by the table.

He turned around, and I saw two tears as big as seeds on the edges of his eyes. "I hate it!"

"Why?"

"There's nothing for me to do except work for Daddy. He's always after me. Do this, do that."

"What's it like when you're here with your mother?"

"She doesn't make me work. She just sits and cries about things like having to go to town to get the newspaper. It's not a real town," he added. "There's nothing there."

"Maybe you can do something nice with your father," I suggested.

"He hates me," David said.

"He doesn't hate you."

"Yes, he does. I never do anything right."

"Maybe," I said, "your father had troubles when he was your age, and now it makes him wild to see you going through it again."

"If he felt like that, he wouldn't hit me."

I put my hand on David's shoulder and kissed the top of his head. His hair smelled slightly sour.

Tom came in from the outside. "Look what I found lying in

the grass." He whipped a saw out from behind his back; the blade looked rusty.

Lenny was in the living room, keeping quiet. David turned away.

"I want to know who is responsible for leaving this saw out in the rain," Tom said.

David ran out of the room.

"Why don't you leave him alone?" I asked as Tom started after him.

He turned back. "He has to learn sometime. His mother still treats him like a baby."

"Try leaving him alone."

"I do leave him alone."

From the living room, Lenny said mildly, "No, you don't, Pop. You're always after him about something—how he's too fat, or he can't read."

"I'm only telling him the truth," Tom said.

"The trouble is, he loves you," I told him.

"What's that got to do with it?"

"Come outside a minute."

"What do you want to say?" Tom asked when we were standing in the circle of light from the porch bulb.

"Try to understand him," I said.

"He's always sniveling."

"I know he's not appealing, but what can he do? He adores you. Lenny—your cool competent son—keeps his distance, and you think it's another sign of superiority."

"Oh, stop," Tom said.

"Watch out, I may turn out to be as bad as David— overweight, demanding, in tears."

"Okay, Caroline."

"Promise me you'll be nice to him, just for this evening."

Tom frowned.

I opened the door then and we went into the kitchen where the tiny chicken was hissing in the oven and the two boys were waiting.

AT SEVEN A.M., in the thick of sleep, I heard a shout, and something crashed on the other side of the wall, near my head. Tom muttered and buried his face in the pillow. "What's going on?" I called. The wall separated Tom's room from his sons'.

In a while I heard scraping and snuffling outside our door. I opened it; David stood on the sill, his pajamas separating to show his sad round belly. "Lenny threw me out."

"He wet the bed!" Lenny shouted, barricaded behind their bedroom door. "It stinks in here!"

"He put my hand in a glass of water while I was asleep," David explained, grinding tears out of his eyes with his fists. "He's done it about a hundred times."

"Tee hee!" Lenny shouted, and I heard him bouncing on the bed.

I knocked, hard, on their door.

Subdued, Lenny called, "Is that you, Pop?"

"I'll get him if you don't unlock this door."

The door opened promptly. Lenny stood zipping up his jeans. "Did we wake you?" he asked politely.

I took hold of his ear, under a shelf of hair. "Apologize to your little brother."

He reached up to feel my fingers. "What for?"

"He says you put his hand in a glass of water."

"That's just a joke."

"It's not a joke if it makes him wet the bed."

"He wets the bed anyway. That's why he couldn't go to camp last summer."

David leapt on his back.

"Get off me!" Lenny shrieked, guarding his face with his hands.

I separated them with difficulty. David had sunk his teeth into his brother's shoulder. "Wait till Pop sees this!" Lenny cried, showing me a round red welt.

"Your father is not going to see it." I handed him a shirt. "You provoked David. Let's go down and see what we can find for breakfast."

I was cracking eggs into a bowl when Tom came in. He poured himself a large glass of orange juice, then drained it. Staring at his sons, he asked, "What was all that noise?"

"We're eating breakfast," I reminded him.

Tom slung himself into a kitchen chair.

"It's a beautiful morning," I went on, looking out the window over the stove. The trees were bare, and the little yard was thick with yellow leaves. A picnic table and a swing set were stranded in the tall weeds.

"I want to know what happened," Tom said. He was looking at Lenny.

Lenny said, "David wet the bed again."

"He put my hand in a glass of water!"

"Never mind that," Tom said. "Did you wet the bed?"

"It was an accident," I told him.

Tom glanced at me.

"Please let it pass," I said.

Tom's look hovered, and then changed. He turned to David. "What's the problem, Son?" he asked. David had started snuffling again.

"Lenny took my binoculars last night and broke them."

"Did not!" Lenny screamed.

"Can't you two leave each other alone?" Tom asked.

Lenny stood up from the table. "I'll leave the asshole alone, Pop," he said carefully. "I'll leave everyone alone." With the dignity of a defeated chieftain, he stalked out of the kitchen.

I refilled Tom's coffee cup. He turned—he was sitting down—and put his arms around me, burying his face in my stomach. David hurried out of the room.

"That boy kills me," Tom said. "He's just like his mother, a zero, a nothing. He can't do anything and he won't even try. He hangs on me and I think he knows it annoys me. I feel sorry for him but it makes me mad just to look at him, those big eyes always wanting something."

"But he loves you," I said.

Tom laughed and let me go. "You foolish people who love me. I do the best I can to make you stop."

"It's a little more complicated than that. Last night you turned over in your sleep and put your arms around me."

He grimaced.

"Yes—you did."

He stood up and emptied his coffee into the sink. "I've got to get snow tires put on the truck. Alice never will take care of anything like that. Lenny!"

The boy appeared in the doorway.

"Want to go to town with me?"

Lenny grabbed his jacket. "Are we going to take David?"

Tom did not answer. He went out the door and, from the window, I saw him hesitate and half turn back. Then he went on to the truck.

I began to wash the dishes. After a while, David came in and hovered at my elbow. I gave him a dish towel.

"Did they go to town?" he asked, slowly drying a plate.

"Yes."

"To go shopping?"

"To have snow tires put on the truck."

"I bet Lenny gets to buy something. He always gets to buy something—at least a candy bar. It's because we don't see Daddy that much," he explained. "All divorced dads buy things, to make up, but he gets a lot more things for Lenny."

"You see him every other weekend," I reminded him, scraping out the skillet. "That's a lot."

"Yeah, but when we stay with him in town, he's always going to parties."

I turned on the tap. David waited until I turned it off and then went on, "And then he comes home late and wakes me up. He nearly always brings some girl."

"Will you do me a favor?" I asked. "The garbage pail is full. Take it out."

"They don't collect on Saturdays."

"You're very like your father sometimes."

"Lenny's like Daddy. I'm like my mom."

"You act just like him." I dried the last plate and put it on the shelf. "Are you going to take out the garbage?"

"Okay," he said and with a great show of effort, he hoisted the pail and carried it out the door.

I went into the living room and sat down. Sunlight fell across the sofa, which looked as though it had been gored; great slits gaped in the arms, and the cushions were leaking. I stood up and began to tidy the place, and then sat down down on an ottoman by the fireplace. Suddenly, I was so tired.

When David came in, I asked him where they kept the firewood.

"In the basement," he said, letting his teeth chatter; he'd gone outside without his jacket. After a long hesitation, he asked if I wanted him to bring some up.

"That would be nice."

He stumped down the basement stairs and came back up with three logs and some kindling in his arms.

"Do you know how to lay a fire?" I asked.

He nodded, and squatted down on the hearth to ball up some newspaper. He laid the balls carefully in the grate, then piled kindling on top. The logs were balanced last, one on top of two. "Who taught you?" I asked.

"Daddy. A long time ago. I made it wrong once and it smoked and he gave the job to Lenny."

He struck a match and pushed it into the paper. "Catch!" he whispered.

The paper twisted and a small flame touched the kindling. A splinter caught and burned. Suddenly there was a rush of flames in front of the logs, and smoke billowed into the room.

"It's smoking!" David cried.

I took a sheet of newspaper and spread it across the fireplace opening.

"I used to do this with my grandmother's fires," I told him.

"It always smokes," he said dubiously.

"Maybe there's something wrong with the flue."

"No," he said soberly. "I didn't do it right. I just threw everything in."

I took the newspaper away. A last puff of smoke disappeared into the room. The fire was burning brightly.

"Do you think it'll still be burning when they get back?" he asked.

"If you feed it. Get some more wood, small stuff."

He stumped down to the basement. Coming back with another load, he said, "It's really burning!"

We both admired it.

We looked up when the door opened. "I smell smoke," Tom said.

"It's not smoking now," I told him. "Come and see." And I held out my hand.

He took it gingerly. "David, I thought I told you not to start fires when I wasn't around."

"Just look how well it's doing," I said.

Tom sat down beside me on the hassock, and David moved out of the way so his father could see the fire.

Lenny came in. "I got a chocolate bar," he told us.

Tom took the poker and made a minute adjustment to the largest log. Glancing at David, he said, "It's a pretty good fire."

Then the four of us sat admiring it, and for the first time that weekend, no one had anything to say.

THAT WINTER

That winter she was living in a cabin in Southern Colorado where the snow came early and stayed late. Once or twice a week, she skied two miles to town for supplies and mail because her pickup had a weak battery and she thought she should save what energy it had for emergencies. (Later, he would tell her the pickup should have been started every day.) She hardly noticed when she began to be watched—a slight woman of no particular age, wearing a rusty-looking black jacket, moving along easily on old, long skis; she had red hair she wore loose under her knitted cap.

At the cabin she developed a routine, writing from sunup until the middle of the morning—she was finishing a novel—cooking with butane (the guy who refilled her tank liked to chat, which wasted time), reading at night by the light of a kerosene lamp. She didn't have guests.

When toward the end of January the nights grew very cold, she began to keep a pile of firewood and kindling by the stove. She didn't split the wood herself, having a healthy respect for axes; there was a man in town who came up and split logs from the pile in the woodshed. He liked to talk, as well.

The logs stacked by the stove meant she didn't have to go out to the woodshed in the middle of the night when the fire had died and the cabin began to freeze. The stars at that time of year have a diamond sharpness; now and then her dog started up from under her bed, barking at coyotes, and she saw those stars through the narrow window that faced her bed.

She had lived another life and sometimes a letter came from that remote time. Standing in the post office in a pool of melting snow, she would study the handwriting on the envelope. Often she tore it up unopened and dropped it in the trash. Eva Williams who was postmistress then noticed and thought it odd; most people, in winter especially, were greedy for mail and saved every scrap. She mentioned it to her husband, Earl, who ran the Chevron, and he passed the observation on to a couple of his regular customers.

No one was much interested. The Southern Rockies were filling up with people whose doings were more colorful than Helen Levant's.

People believed she had been married to a lot of money at

one time, but all marriages went to hell eventually, especially in the big cities. It seemed there were no children.

Actually her story was different. Not much given to introspection, she'd told friends in Philadelphia she was going to "light out for the territory" on a whim, but it had been a strong whim, an impulse of the first magnitude. Now she was beginning to feel its fading, especially in the evening when her writing was done—she set herself a daily number of words—and the book she was reading seemed unlikely to hold her interest.

There was nowhere to go. The town bar held no attraction, and she was, in any event, not reckless enough to ski down the road in the dark. So she stayed put, telling herself an occasional bout of loneliness was the price she paid for freedom.

One evening toward the end of February when she was talking on the telephone to an old friend (she did keep in touch with a few people), someone knocked on her door. With the cordless phone in one hand, she went to see who it was.

A couple was standing on her doorstep in the glare of headlights. The man said, blearily, "We need help," and the woman groaned, clutching her stomach. Because of the woman, Helen let them in.

She told her friend she'd call back and hung up. Turning, she was astonished to see the couple seated at her kitchen table.

(Later, the friend, who'd been Helen's editor at one point,

said she'd thought it strange when Helen didn't call her back. She knew Helen was scrupulous, especially about social obligations.)

Helen stared at the two strangers seated at her table. The woman was vastly pregnant; her stomach jutted out of her coat and rested on her knees. Her legs were bare, and she was wearing bedraggled pink slippers with pompons on the toes. Helen saw a splash of blood on her left calf.

The man was a little older and rougher, the flaps of his cap pulled down over his ears, his hands encased in big canvas mittens that looked like lobster claws; he pulled one off and offered Helen a hand that was large and surprisingly warm.

"Ran out of gas, got to get her to the hospital," he said, at which the woman let out a strangled moan. "It's coming fast."

"My truck isn't running," Helen said.

The woman moaned again and bent down until her forehead was on the table. Helen saw the nape of her neck, plain and bare. Her hair was screwed up with bobby pins.

"Drain off some gas?" the man asked, getting up and going to the door with her keys in hand.

Helen snatched her jacket and followed, protesting. Later she would say her protests were feeble. The woman was right behind her, moaning. The man walked right by his own car as though he hadn't noticed that the headlights were on and the doors hanging open.

He started Helen's pickup on the first try.

Of course Helen had to go with them then. What choice did she have? The woman was about to give birth; she'd just crouched down in a puddle of liquid.

Helen took the woman's arm and pushed her up into the truck, and then climbed in beside her. The three of them were uncomfortably crowded, thigh to thigh, and the woman was still moaning.

There began one of Helen's strangest rides. Not the strangest, she'd claim later. That was the time, years earlier, when Ben Levant, her then-husband, had threatened to drive them both off the pier in Key West. The top of the red convertible had been down—it was midnight, Ben was drunk—and Helen had thought she could swim out once the car was submerged. But then he'd driven back to their hotel, quite quietly.

At the hospital, they stopped at the emergency room door, and two men rushed out with a stretcher on wheels. They rolled the woman onto it expertly while Helen stood holding the door. When she looked across the empty seat at the man, he was staring straight ahead.

"Get out," Helen said. The stretcher was already inside the emergency room.

"She's okay now, nothing I can do," he muttered.

"You can't just leave her," Helen said firmly.

"She's not mine."

"What!" Helen exclaimed. "Where'd you find her?"

He looked at her. "Hitching," he said. "I saw she was in trouble."

Helen thought it might be a con. She was a sophisticated woman, after all, who had spent most of her life in big cities. But he hadn't asked for money and so she couldn't imagine what he might want, other than a ride to the hospital, and now, inevitably, a ride back to her house to get his car.

She thought of taking over the driving, but it would require an effort; his hands were clamped on her steering wheel. So she climbed in beside him—he hadn't cut the motor—and they rode back in silence.

At her house, he thanked her and turned to his car, the doors still hanging open, the headlights on. There was something forlorn about the old hulk waiting there in the cold; certainly it wouldn't start—which was why, Helen would explain later, she invited him in for coffee.

Methodically, he turned off the headlights, closed the door, and followed her inside.

By now it was very late, and she felt the oddness of being alone with a stranger in the middle of the night. "I haven't been up this late for years," she said, realizing that she sounded girlish.

And so it was inevitable that he would put his hands on her

hips from behind as she stood grinding the coffee beans. She hadn't even known he was standing that close.

Turning, she looked at him. He was smiling.

"Now," she said, and she heard her mother's voice. It was a warning more to herself than to him. She followed that with "Now what?" which was not what she'd intended to say.

"Now what we both want," he said into her neck, and he kissed the sensitive spot under her ear.

Not her shoulder; not her cheek. It had taken Ben months to find that particular place.

In the morning she woke up first and took a shower; the water was nearly cold because the overcast had diminished her solar. Shivering, wrapped in a towel, she went back to her bedroom with the intention of rousing him and sending him on his way. But he was already awake, looking at her.

"Come on back," he said. "It's too cold to get up this early."

And so she went.

An intelligent woman, she would tell herself later, a woman who'd had plenty of experience with men, men of her class and background and education, who knew how to deal with flirts, and worse, knew how to stop hands and lips and even tongues when that was called for—and there she was, at seven in the morning, lying beneath the considerable bulk of a man whose name she didn't know.

It was Danny, or Dan, she found out.

Finally she sat up abruptly and scrabbled for her watch on the nightstand. She couldn't believe it was almost ten. "I never sleep this late," she said. "I have work to do."

"You weren't sleeping."

"Yes I was, and so were you!" she cried indignantly.

He didn't answer. His back was turned to her, his bare arm hooked over his face; she realized she'd never really seen him. It had been dark the night before, and there had hardly been time, this morning.

"I don't know you," she said briskly. "I think you'd better go."

He took her in his arms again. She had to admit to herself that it had been years since she'd aroused such enthusiasm.

What does knowing matter, she wondered at noon when she was fixing them both grilled cheese sandwiches. (He didn't like the mustard, which was flavored with wine.) The kind of knowing she'd credited for her marriage and her affairs hadn't meant much; it had worn through and blown away with the first disagreement. How, she'd often wondered, could a man change so fast, over the course of a few hours or days, from the person she'd found charming, interesting, possibly worthwhile, to something glowering or glum, silent, unreachable?

But this man, this Danny, told her nothing. He had long legs, broad shoulders, and he wore the corny heart-printed cotton boxers she'd seen once in a catalogue; he'd pulled them on to eat his grilled cheese sandwich.

She found herself glancing at his chest. It was smooth, hairless, and his nipples were pale lavender.

"Do you do this often?" she asked, pouring each of them a glass of milk. She was able to prevent herself from saying that she hadn't had a glass of milk in decades.

He shook his head, chewing.

Then she was afraid he was married. But he said he wasn't. "Divorced," he added in a matter-of-fact voice, just the voice, Helen realized, she would like to use to explain her own situation.

He sat at the kitchen table for a while, and then finished dressing—his jeans were worn but they fit well, and his flannel shirt was a washed-out pink—and told her he'd "be on his way." He lingered for a moment in the doorway, and she realized she wanted him to stay.

And so she asked him to.

She was, as she knew, a sophisticated woman who'd lived most of her life in big cities, etcetera. But she asked him to stay, and he did.

There began the strangest episode in Helen's life and, as she admitted to herself, it was a life that had not lacked for strangeness. (How else would she have been able to face a winter alone in an unheated cabin in the southern Rockies?)

They were not happy together, nor were they unhappy. He left early, usually; he worked on a construction site, and now and then the foreman would call at six A.M. and say the job was off for the day because of the cold. Then Danny would go back to bed, and Helen would, as well.

On Fridays, he usually brought home a couple of bags of groceries—chips and canned salsa and beer and frozen dinners; Helen accepted this as her due and even began to enjoy the unfamiliar flavors. He didn't smoke, and his drinking was confined to those couple of beers on Friday night. He wasn't interested in television, the movies were too far away, and when Helen read in the evenings, he usually dozed. But he was wide awake at ten when they went to bed.

Since there was nothing to talk about, Helen realized, there was nothing to quarrel about. The cabin was nearly as silent as it had been when she was alone. The only new sounds were the whine of his electric razor and the bang of his car door. On Saturday mornings, he liked to listen to a radio program about fixing cars; Helen found it quite amusing, too.

"I wonder what happened to that pregnant woman," she asked him one evening after about a month, over hamburgers he'd bought at a fast-food place on his way home. Hers was nearly cold, and the bun was thin and damp.

"I guess she's had that baby by now," he said, smiling.

"Maybe we ought to check," she said on the spur of the moment; she was always doing or saying things on the spur of the moment, those days.

He didn't object, and so the next day, after skiing into town for a few essentials (she hardly noticed that she was even more carefully watched than before), Helen called the hospital, and because it was a little local place, she was able to get her questions answered without much trouble.

The woman had given birth within an hour of her arrival to a healthy eight-pound boy.

As soon as she heard that, Helen could see him: the round dumpling child.

"What do babies do when they're a month old?" she asked Danny that evening. He shrugged. "I don't think they do much," she went on, half to herself. "Sleep and eat and shit, that's about it. I wonder if she's breastfeeding." Her vision sharpened as she spoke.

"No, she put him on a bottle right away," she said, her voice cold with indignation. "They told her at the hospital she should breastfeed, but—"

"Hey," Danny said.

"It's the strangest thing—I've been seeing that baby all day," Helen confided doubtfully.

"You mean in your head?"

"Well, yes. It's never happened to me before."

He studied her for a while. "You want to go see them?"

She laughed. It seemed a preposterous suggestion.

"I know how to find her," he added softly.

"You said you didn't know her!"

"I didn't, but I know how to find her."

It was one of the longest conversations they'd had.

A few days later, Danny told her to put on her jacket; they were going to visit the baby.

It was five o'clock, he was just home from work, and Helen had been lighting the stove.

"What in the world——" she said, laughing.

"You said you wanted to see him," he reminded her, standing in the doorway. He hadn't even taken off his coat.

She found herself scrambling into her jacket; he had to remind her to take her hat and gloves.

It was very cold; there were frost spiders on all the windows, and the sun was sinking in bruised violets and pinks.

She followed him into her pickup—it was running reliably now, he'd done something to the battery.

They slid down the hill—the road had melted during the day and was now in the process of freezing—and skidded out onto the highway, which Helen had skied earlier in the day. "Sometimes I wonder about cars," she said. "I mean, why we use them."

He didn't answer.

They drove five or six miles, through the little town and out the other side, where there was a scattering of small houses and trailers. He turned in at a dented mailbox; that was all Helen noticed—a white mailbox with a huge dent in its side, as though it had suffered a direct hit. At the end of a short road, a house with a screened porch stood almost hidden by snow-bowed junipers.

"Is there a husband?" she asked as she scrambled out of the car. "A boyfriend?"

"Nobody I know of," he said, leading the way down the path. It had not been shoveled, and Helen slipped and nearly fell on a patch of ice.

He continued on ahead of her.

At the door, he waited for her to catch up, and then knocked, lightly.

The door opened at once, dislodging a shelf of snow; Danny avoided it. Peering over his shoulder, Helen saw a small, pale woman wearing what used to be called a housedress. She looked so shrunken Helen at first didn't believe it was the same woman, but then she saw she had a baby on her arm.

Helen pushed in front of Danny. "You shouldn't stand out here in the cold with the baby," she said.

Then she led the way into a dark kitchen. The woman was at her heels, and Danny was coming along behind. He closed the kitchen door, and Helen heard another shelf of snow crash to the ground. "You haven't been out in days," she said to the woman. It sounded like an accusation.

"Car's broke," the woman said. She had brown eyes and soft, very pale skin that looked as though it bruised easily; her hair, as long as though she was still a girl, hung loose around her thin shoulders.

Helen was looking at the baby. He was asleep in the crook of the woman's arm. His face was closed as a shell, lips and lids firmly shut as though he'd made a decision to sleep through anything. His pale, transparent ears stuck out almost straight from each side of his head, and what hair he had was thin and pale as gauze.

"You ought to tape his ears back," Helen said, "so they'll lie close to his head."

She reached out and touched one of the baby's ears. It was barely warm, delicate as a petal.

Then she was holding out her arms.

The woman transferred the baby with a sigh. Helen shifted him a little to get him comfortable in the crook of her arm. His eyes stayed closed, but his mouth opened slightly.

"He's yawning! Yawning in his sleep!" Helen said.

After a minute she felt Danny's hand on her arm. "That's enough, now. Hand him back."

She did. The woman—the mother—took the baby without

much sign that it made a difference to her one way or another. "You bring something to eat?" she asked Danny.

He shook his head. "Will, tomorrow. You got anything for supper?"

"Some tuna."

"What about the baby? What is the baby going to eat?" Helen asked in distress.

"I feed him myself," the woman said with modest pride.

Now Helen noticed that her breasts were swollen inside her housedress, which was stained down the front.

"He eats a lot—little pig," the woman said, jostling the baby.

"Be careful," Helen warned her. "I read you can hurt their brains if you shake them."

"That wasn't shaking," the woman said, looking at her suspiciously.

"That's enough, now," Danny said again, and he took Helen's hand and guided her to the door.

The woman turned on the porch light.

"You think she's telling the truth? You think she's got enough milk for him?" Helen asked as Danny led the way to the pickup. "If the mother doesn't eat right, her milk dries up."

"That baby's doing fine," Danny said, and for the first time, he opened the passenger door of the pickup and waited while Helen pulled herself in.

While he walked around to the driver's side, she strained to see through the lighted kitchen window.

"We'll come back tomorrow with some groceries, right?" she asked Danny as soon as he was seated beside her. "Something healthy, broccoli maybe, for her. And for the baby, what? A baby that age doesn't eat solids, does he? I wonder if he's teething—would he chew on teething biscuits?"

Danny patted her hand. "He's way too young for that."

"How do you know? You never had any children, either," she said judiciously.

"I ever tell you that?" When she didn't answer, too stunned to form a word, he said, "Because if I did, it was a lie. I got a boy and a girl, almost grown, over in Trinidad."

She was so surprised and so pained she could hardly breathe.

"I don't see them much, their mother don't like me," he added, as though that would make her feel better.

"I never knew," she gasped.

"Now, Honey—" he patted her hand again.

"You never call me Honey," she said. "You never call me anything. Sometimes I think you don't know my name."

He laughed. She could see his lips in the light from the dashboard.

"Don't laugh," she said. "I don't know what's happening to me," she added.

"I know what's happening to you," he said, and he glanced quickly at her.

"Well, then, tell me," she said.

THE BIG NO

Forty years ago it had been so easy just to crash wherever he happened to be late at night. There was always a couch or his sleeping bag on the floor. The people of the house did not notice him when they got up in the morning to make coffee and get ready to leave for a job or drive a child to school.

He spent the night at some woman's house. He couldn't remember who she'd been. She had thrown a big party and he'd stayed late because of a girl he was talking to who seemed like a possibility. He'd thought she might invite him to spend the night with her, but somehow she drifted off and disappeared without that happening.

Before he sacked out on the woman's floor, Jules put his diary on the table near where he'd spread his sleeping bag. It was a lined notebook he'd been writing in most days since he left home and hit the road. The diary was full of bits and pieces—notes, phone numbers, descriptions of girls he'd met.

Their remoteness had done nothing to diminish his ardor. He tried to analyze those meetings and their participants because he was troubled by the intensity of his desire for girls who seemed far away from him in all ways. He'd never gone further than kissing, and he thought it was his own suspicion of his desire that stopped developments, rather than the girls' hesitations, although those certainly played a role.

Late at night after one of these encounters, he would write, "Nice boobs, a little small, though, under that tight blue T-shirt. Pretty hair all the way down to her waist, she looked like she was dressed in it. She smiled, I thought she was smiling at me, but maybe at somebody over my shoulder. We talked about her trip to India, the guru she met, how he changed her life. I believed her but didn't know how to say it, not that it would have mattered. She left around midnight, I didn't see her go. Named Lucy but I don't know anything more."

Another time, when things had gone a little further, he wrote, "When we were sitting in my car, she let me put my hand up between her thighs. Nice and moist. She mewed a little. I wanted to unzip, I was hard as a rock, but when I took my hand away to undo my zipper she pulled her legs together and got out of the car.

THE BIG NO

Did I say something? Don't know. May try to call her tomorrow, get together for coffee, move more slowly. Maybe I scared her? Don't think so, though. Remember to get more condoms, the one in my wallet is dried up." (His older brother had given him his first condom and insisted on showing him how to put it on, in spite of Jules' embarrassment which had amounted almost to rage.)

Girls were the main but not the only things he wrote about in his diary. He described the hikes he'd taken in Colorado earlier in the summer—he'd climbed three fourteeners—and his plans to go to France and hitchhike around in the fall. He wrote a little about his family but not much because he was trying to stop brooding about them. His stepfather had kicked him out of the house five months earlier and since then Jules hadn't seen his family, although he talked to his mom now and then on the phone.

He couldn't understand why she'd married that jerk after all those years when she seemed to be perfectly happy working and raising her kids. He guessed she was worried now about old age and security. The jerk had money and could take her places she'd never been able to afford before—they were cruising in Greece right at the moment. Jules felt a flash of anger at the thought of Greece when he was sleeping on people's floors most of the time and not even able to score, but then he tried to distract himself with thoughts of the girl he'd met most recently, who'd let him put his hand between her thighs.

"A girl who would do that would do a lot more," he wrote in his diary before he went to sleep that night on the woman's floor.

When he woke up it was morning and the house seemed to be empty. He got up and pulled on his shirt and pants, rolled up his sleeping bag, and grabbed his guitar. Then he eased himself out of the house, closing the door without a sound—he was practiced in that—and went to his car.

The old heap started with a lot of noise but he'd parked some distance from the house because of the crowd the night before and so he thought the noise wouldn't bother anybody if there was anybody to be bothered. He drove into town to get coffee and when he was drinking it he remembered he had left his diary.

The front door had locked behind him when he left and probably there would be nobody to let him in. He planned to wait until evening when the woman or somebody else would be there. He was uncomfortable at the thought of his diary lying naked and exposed on the woman's table, but there didn't seem to be anything to do about it. He reasoned that there was nobody in the house, not even a dog, and who would be interested in his diary anyway?

There was a plaza in the middle of the small Southwestern town and he decided to go there and hang out. He'd ended up in this particular town because someone he met in Denver had mentioned a job with his uncle who ran a garage. The job hadn't panned out because the uncle was out of town and the man who was in charge at the garage said he had no authority to hire anyone—which was probably just as well, Jules thought, since what he knew about cars would fit into a small cup.

He was a musician by vocation (that was one of the things the jerk had held against him, the "noise" he made playing drums and the fact, which could never be argued against, that drumming would never pay his bills) and so he went to the plaza, hoping maybe to find some musicians who would know about possible bands and venues, even in a small town. If that didn't happen, he would have to leave as soon as he retrieved his diary.

The plaza was green and plush with a pretty bandstand in the middle. There were some kids sitting around, talking and smoking. Jules was shy by nature and it helped that one of the kids had a dog, since he could go up to a dog and start a conversation.

This dog had a cat sitting on its back and a mouse on top of the cat and was employed for panhandling, pretty successfully, the kid in charge of the trio told him. Jules was not allowed to pat the dog or even to talk to him, since it would distract him from focusing on his job, which was to keep the cat on his back and the mouse on top of the cat, although Jules didn't understand how the dog's concentration could have any effect on the other two animals. The cat was cowering on the dog's spine and the mouse quivered on top of the cat with a terrible alertness. But he was willing to give the theory the benefit of the doubt, especially after he saw the expression in the dog's yellow eyes. He was concentrating, there was no doubt about it, and Jules realized he had never seen a dog concentrate before.

He hung out for a while with the group and got some pretty useful information. There was a youth hostel out on the strip with a place to spend the night if he could come up with five dollars, which didn't seem impossible, and a soup kitchen that was free. The food would be terrible but so what. Jules, who had never been particularly aware of soup kitchens or hostels when he was living at home, was grateful for them now and even amazed that they existed, although it shamed him that the soup kitchens were meant to support down-and-out, drugged, drunk, or crazed low-lifes.

At noon he drove over to the soup kitchen with a girl named Wendy who seemed to like him and who was sort of pretty if you could get beyond the big snake tattooed on her right arm. It ran from her shoulder to her wrist and curled around her elbow. Jules' eyes kept going there. He couldn't imagine how the girl had endured the pain such a big tattoo would have caused.

She seemed glad to show him where the soup kitchen was and to keep him company in the line that had formed outside the door. Since she was clean and sort of pretty having her there in the line beside him made it seem, Jules thought, that he was not a part of the regular clientele. Which was exactly the clientele he'd encountered in Denver and Helena and Albuquerque, as though whatever form of street life existed in those places sprang from the same hidden root.

They ate thick brown bean soup, the specialty of those places, for which Jules had to remind himself to be grateful. The clouds had burned off and it had turned hot; a cold soup or a salad would have been more welcome. He had no hat and Wendy said he was too fair to be out in that sun unprotected; she rubbed sunblock on his face, giggling as though her knowledge of him ran more than skin deep. That bothered Jules and he decided to dump her as soon as the meal was finished.

After they'd scraped their plates and piled them, he found himself watching her leave, sort of annoyed because she hadn't said goodbye or told him where she was heading. She had a cute little rear end and he thought he would write about that when he had his diary, which reminded him that he needed to go back and get it before too long.

He spent the afternoon walking along the old railroad tracks that had once linked the town with its bigger neighbor. The railroad tracks were overrun with chamisa and ironweed, and gophers popped into their holes as he passed. The thin shade of the weed trees did not protect him from the sun, and he was so thirsty he stooped to drink out of a hose, which he had never done before. The hose was lying in a small yard that edged the tracks and while he was drinking out of it, a big dog rushed barking out of the house and attacked him and he had to run, wondering if someone had let the dog out on purpose. Tracks were always full of homeless men wandering back and forth and he made a decision then and there to avoid them in the future.

The encounter with the dog depressed him because it reminded him of the worst night, the first he'd spent on the road, before he learned how to handle the situation. Dark had come on, he'd had no money, and he was only a few miles from home, but of course he couldn't go back. Finally he'd come to an abandoned house, one of those shacks you sometimes see beside a cornfield in the deep country. As though it was a real house, he'd gone up and knocked on the door but there was no one inside and there hadn't been anyone inside for many years.

It had turned very cold when the sun set. He'd walked around the shack, its siding gray and peeling, broken cars and tractors and piles of trash scattered through the long weeds. There'd been an old bathtub stranded out there, and he'd thought of trying to sleep in it but the cold was growing intense and he knew his summer-weight sleeping bag wouldn't do it.

Finally he'd seen a slat missing from one of the boarded up windows, and he wrenched it off and then the other slats, pushed up the window and climbed in. The room he'd entered had smelled of piss and long-dead ashes, and the only piece of furniture had been a filthy, stoved-in couch. He'd had to lie on it because the floor was even filthier, and he was afraid of rats or some such things. He knew his mother would have cried if she'd seen him huddled on that couch, his sleeping bag zipped to the chin to keep out everything that could be kept out, but the thought of her crying had not comforted him. If she had stood up for him when the jerk insulted him, instead of lurking in the kitchen, sobbing, he would have been at home now in his own clean bed. Women's tears weren't worth anything unless they resulted in some profitable action.

There had been no dog in the shack but the dog lunging at him earlier along the tracks reminded him of that night, of what it felt like, the first time, to be outside of protection, to be alone in a way he'd never been alone before, in his big, squabbling family. He'd hadn't even had his own room—or wanted it.

He tried to turn off his depression as you would turn off a faucet (sometimes that actually worked) and when that didn't help he decided to go back to his car and drive out to the woman's house and retrieve his diary. At least he could find somewhere to sit before it got dark and write his description of Wendy with her big, off-putting snake tattoo and her cute rear end.

He had some difficulty finding the right street since all the neighborhoods on the edge of the town looked alike, yards with a pad of bluegrass kept alive with busy sprinklers and front doors hedged with flowers. It was the time of the evening when people were outside, leaving the air conditioners and televisions behind for a few minutes between sunset and true dark. Some children were riding bikes and a couple of adults were standing talking on the corner. They stared at his car apprehensively as though they could tell from its appearance he had no business there. He looked straight ahead and drove carefully, and eventually he found the woman's house.

By now there were lights on and he felt uneasy as he approached, wondering if she would remember him. It had been a big party and he wasn't sure he'd even spoken to the hostess. He wondered if he was forgetting how to act, as though that was another part of his old life that had slipped away along with daily showers and shaving and hot breakfasts and his mother's hand on his shoulder.

He rang the bell. It played a tune on the other side of the door, a sweet jingling that repelled him.

After a while he heard footsteps and the door opened a little. Light fell out in a long blade and he felt tempted to cover his face. The woman was standing there staring at him, and suddenly Jules knew she did remember him although he was not sure her memory was a pleasant one.

"Excuse me for bothering you," he said, "but I left something last night in your living room."

"Yes, you did," she said, still staring at him. She was older than he remembered, almost old enough to be his mother, and she was dressed in jeans that were too tight around her thick thighs and a cardigan that looked as though it had been washed many times. Above the cardigan her face was narrow and suspicious and he thought she was not going to ask him to come in.

"It's my diary," he said, as though that would soften her.

"I know."

Finally she opened the door a little wider and stepped aside, and he took that for an invitation and went in.

One lamp was turned on in the living room and he heard a television chattering in the corner.

His diary was where he had left it, on a small round table.

Jules tried to pick it up casually but his anxiety made him grab it with both hands, as though it was a sandwich and he was starving. The diary felt different, heavier, somehow, as though it had soaked up some of the atmosphere of the dark house. "Thank you," he said, although he didn't know what he was thanking her for, and then he stepped quickly to the door. She closed it behind him with a smart click.

She hadn't said a word to him between the time she let him in the house and the time he found his diary and left. He thought that was quite unfriendly and wondered if she had not planned on returning the diary to him or if she was in the midst of some kind of personal crisis that made her cranky.

Red Car

In the end it meant nothing to him. He would never see her again. He carried the diary to his car with an extra consideration for its added heft and got in, laying the diary on the seat beside him. It was full dark now and he decided to go back to the plaza and write up the day's notes before finding the hostel and settling down for the night.

The plaza was deserted and he was glad to find a bench under a bright light. It was chilly but he was wearing his leather jacket and he did not feel the cold too much.

He opened the diary on his knee. As he leafed through the pages, he felt satisfied with the amount he had written; he had hardly skipped a day since he left home. The ink changed colors and sometimes he even wrote in pencil, but the pages were evenly and steadily filled and he felt he was keeping a worthy record. In time to come when his circumstances improved, he would keep the diary in a special place and reread bits of it when he needed a lesson in gratitude. By then he believed he would have a steady girl and perhaps she would enjoy his descriptions of the girls he had met along the way. She would be the kind of girl who understood that all the others had been merely stepping-stones leading him to her.

He reread what he'd written the day before when he was at a truck stop on the north side of town. It was not one of the more interesting entries since nothing had happened that day; just a routine trip from Denver south. There hadn't been any untoward delays or odd meetings and he had not even glimpsed a girl. Still he had written conscientiously about the weather and the way he had felt, which had been pretty good, considering.

Since his main object in writing the diary was to analyze girls, he'd spent half of that page on the girl he'd met in Denver, the one who'd let him put his hand between her thighs. He'd described her thin blond hair that fell down over her shoulders and her blue eyes and her snub nose that made her look about ten years old. And then he saw something on the opposite page, the page that should have been empty, waiting for his next entry.

It hadn't been written on, he realized, it was still fresh and blank, but over its freshness and blankness a carefully cut out piece of red paper had been laid. It was just the right size to cover the blank page of his diary. In the middle of the red paper, a very large, very black two-letter word had been inked in:

NO

Jules stared at the word. It had been written carefully, each letter dark and measured and black, and the red paper around it meticulously scalloped, so that it almost seemed pleasant in its intention, like an invitation or a valentine.

But then he realized that the word was a blow. It struck him where he was tender and exposed, and he began to sweat as he stared at it. The woman had picked up his diary and decided to answer him, to contradict what he'd thought when the diary was his, and private.

He imagined going back to the house, hammering on the door and demanding to know why she had done such a thing, why she had trespassed on his freedom. But then he knew it would do no good. She had spent time and care on that one word, and she would defend it with many words, carefully chosen to make her point. He did not want to feel that point pressing into his face. In fact he was already feeling the point. It stuck into him as though she had pushed it with all her strength into his flesh.

NO

As he stared at the word, he realized that she had not defaced his diary. She had inserted something he could immediately remove. He took out the piece of red paper and thought of crumpling or tearing it and throwing it in a garbage can. It would be gone in a couple of seconds. He could close his diary, get up, and find somewhere to spend the night. He need never think about it again.

But now he found himself studying the word as though its message was beginning to unfold. The word seemed to consist of many layers. The layers unfurled as he stared. The *no* was a *no* but also it was an invitation (not a valentine), and he wanted to know, suddenly, what the word invited him into, what the door was that the woman he didn't know and would never know had opened for him. He thought no one had ever written so carefully to him and he wondered why she had cared.

He went back to the previous page and read what he had written about the willing girl in Denver, and he understood now that the *no* was a response to that description.

Turning to a fresh page, he realized that an edge of red paper stuck out, and that it would stick out from all the subsequent pages, all the way to the end of the diary, which was still far off. Every time he made an entry, he would see that margin of red and know the *no* was hidden there, waiting.

Now he wanted to write his usual entry but he did not know what to say. The day had been rich in incidents and he should have been able to fill up at least several paragraphs if not more. Yet he could not begin. He sat with his ballpoint in his hand and stared at the bare sheet, which seemed to flicker under the hard blue streetlight.

He imagined the woman crossing her living room to the small round table and seeing his diary lying there. He imagined her hesitating before picking it up, but then reminding herself that the thing had been left in her house and she had every right to examine it.

As she opened it, he knew she would have considered reading every page, out of simple curiosity.

Possibly she would have read the few pages while standing

there, his diary balanced in one hand, the other on her hip. Possibly at the end of those few pages, she would have closed the diary and stared at the wall. An expression of some kind would have crossed her face, but Jules did not know what that expression would have been.

Then she would have gone to the closet where she kept paper and such and without any hesitation, she would have chosen the sheet of red paper and the scissors that made scallops and the black marker pen that made a thick, dense line.

He imagined her going into her kitchen and sitting down at the table there, pushing some glasses and an ashtray to one side. She might have leaned her chin on her hand for just a moment before she began to cut, but after she began, she would not have stopped. When the piece of paper was prepared, she would have taken the black marker and begun, very carefully, to write the N. She would have outlined it first and then filled in the outline with broad strokes. When the N was completed to her satisfaction, she would have started on the O. And when both letters were formed and the black ink had dried, she would have looked at her work with satisfaction before closing it inside his diary.

She had known he would come for it, sooner or later, and she had known she would give it to him without a word.

As he sat there bewildered, not knowing what to do, Jules remembered the only time he'd surprised his mother and her suitor in the kitchen. It happened a few weeks before the man told him to leave. The man was holding Jules' mother by the waist and burying his face in her neck, under her brown hair. As the man nuzzled her neck, Jules' mother was staring fixedly. When she saw her son stop at the door to the kitchen, she formed a word with her lips which she did not speak.

No, her lips formed, and he saw the word and understood it and passed on upstairs.

Her *no* was not kin to the *no* in his diary and yet his acceptance of the one seemed to lead to his acceptance of the other. His mother's *no* was provisional, it would never be formed again. The no in Jules' diary would be there forever, repeating and repeating itself, whether he destroyed the red paper or even the diary itself (which he did not think he would ever write in again). Yet what mattered more than his shame and even his anger was the curious relief he also felt, like a small breeze through an open door.

SWEET PEAS

At a cafe not far from the Sorbonne, a couple is sitting in the August crowd. They are Americans—anyone can see that—comfortably if casually dressed, their hands folded around their demitasse cups in the proprietary way Americans have. They are wedged in at their small table—both are tall—by the knees and elbows of people at the adjoining tables placed along the narrow stretch of concrete.

The woman reaches out during a silence in the conversation and touches the ordinary bright red geranium blooming in a wooden planter at her knee.

The silence is not long, it is not profound, it is the silence that occurs when two people have spent a month together. This silence is made up of the moment before dawn when one of them woke and, turning, found that the bed held the other; a moment not of seeking, yet not of satisfaction, for the body that is found at dawn in the bed is always the body of a stranger, no matter what may have transpired the night before. This silence is also the silence of waiting on train platforms, in airport lounges, where a tinge of anxiety gives the silence texture; it is the silence of waiting to be noticed in the far-too-expensive restaurants they feel obliged to try.

It is his silence—Roland Boyd's silence—when his companion begins to speak French (she speaks well, this Madeline, he admires her for it, yet silence is his only resort at such times since he speaks no French at all), and it is her silence when he reads the *Paris Herald* and seems to disappear. They are old enough, and wise enough, to have arranged various separations, strategically located during their long trip; they do not want "to wear each other out," as Madeline says, "to get dull and staid," as Roland says—they have a horror of the way other Americans travel, or seem to travel, alternating irritation and numbness.

Neither of them would call this trip their honeymoon—they are not married, have no plans to marry, have never even discussed marrying, except obliquely, in terms of other people's mistakes—and yet an impartial observer might assume as much, because of the careful, quiet way Madeline has dressed, even on this hot August day, because of the way her hand strays, now and then, to Roland's on the white tablecloth. And she has, the observer would surely have noted, offered Roland the little white cup of sugar lumps, would—if she hadn't restrained herself — have taken a lump out with the tongs and dropped it in his tiny cup, because he loves sugar and often denies himself.

Madeline, however, does not make this mistake—not this morning, not this hot August morning in the cafe near the Sorbonne—because she is finally coming to understand that her gestures do not summon his, as for a long time she thought or felt they might.

She remembered this when they sat down at the little round table, jammed in with its neighbors, because of the way Roland stared out at once into the street. She knows him so well, this keen observer, that she no longer needs to ask him what he thinks or how he feels. (Sometimes he volunteers this information.) He sat down in the chair, fatigued—they have been walking the neighborhood all morning—with the obliviousness which, she knows, is key to his survival. He has loved once, he has loved deeply—so he has told her—and he does not expect to love in that way again.

Madeline, a realist whose first husband left her early in their marriage, knows that when a man says something about love or the lack of it women should take note, for if a man knows anything at all, he knows his capacity to love, or not, as he knows the interior of his car's engine or the contents of his wallet. Other statements may be open to question——how and why a child rebels, for instance, or what is a suitable way to greet a lover after a break-up——but on the question of love, men are exact. So she has taken note——took note, in fact, the first time they had dinner together——and is always in the process of wrapping her feelings around his. She likes the starkness of his lack because she can festoon it with her own luxuriant emotions, growing morning glories to cover his absence.

She has had, though, an odd moment an hour or so before they sat down. It began when they were walking through the vast church whose name she has already forgotten, when they were admiring the great golden balloon, several stories tall, which some modern artist has placed in the nave. The great balloon reflects on its golden surface the high windows in the chancel; it was beautiful, Roland said, the most beautiful thing he'd seen so far in Paris, and Madeline objected that it was beautiful but so out of place, taking up the entire nave where once people prayed.

"Oh you Catholics," Roland said gently, and since it was a topic they've agreed to avoid, she said nothing.

But the moment stretched itself like a small, sunning snake all the way to the table on the sidewalk. Without that moment, Madeline knows, she would never have noticed the sweet peas.

Paris is full of flowers——it is one of the things she loves about the city——and the sidewalk florist they passed just before they sat down was nothing special, nothing even particularly attractive: a torn canvas awning, a few tubs of flowers, a woman scaling off leaves behind a counter. But in the tubs set closest to the sidewalk, there were sweet peas—lavender, white, and pink.

"Sweet peas!" Madeline said, and Roland, a step or so ahead, nodded without turning around.

But Madeline stopped and leaned down—bent double, almost—to smell the closest bunch. It was pale lavender, the small blooms tied tightly together, the stems swimming in water. A few drops of water clung to the blooms, and Madeline tasted one drop with the tip of her tongue. The water tasted only of coolness but when she breathed in, the sweet pea blossoms had the sharp, small scent that was exactly what she needed, exactly what she came to France to find.

"Sweet peas," she said, again, as she lifted her head but Roland was already negotiating for a chair at the cafe table.

She hurried then to find him. There was a sweatiness in the air, the city air of a long summer, a confusion of people and cars and slightly leaning three-story buildings; the sky seemed blocked, or was it only pale, so pale it could hardly be seen? She did not know as she took the other chair at the table and saw Roland staring at a wall, or a car, or someone else—she did not know, it did not really matter. His eyes were averted.

Now she summons the waiter in her precise, educated

French, the accent not quite right, she knows, but still intelligible, and he brings them two more demitasses of thick coffee which he places beside the cup of sugar cubes and the saucer of lemon rinds.

Then, without being asked, she hands the sugar to Roland and suppresses the impulse to take out the sugar cube and drop it into his coffee.

There are ways and ways of coming to understanding, she will think later, when she reflects on that morning, but surely the moment of understanding that has the highest polish takes place in Paris, derives some of its luster not so much from the place itself—a big city on a hot morning—as from the memories and assumptions that cluster around it.

Roland doesn't thank her for passing the cup of sugar. He is used to her ministrations, as he calls them. Usually she doesn't notice his failure to thank her—how absurd it would be to hold someone who knows her so intimately to such a formality—but today, because of the sweet peas, she does notice. "Why didn't you thank me?" she asks, as frankly as a child.

He replies with a stare and something dismissive. It doesn't matter, she knows, exactly what words come to him at that moment; they are the words that have been waiting for a month like pebbles at the bottom of a well.

"I asked because of the sweet peas," she explains, "and my mother."

SWEET PEAS

She has told Roland, as she tells all her close friends, the story of her mother, which is dim and gray as, it often seems, her mother, who worked hard, who saved money, who had no time, was dim and gray; but the sweet peas are from another compartment, one she's never opened. "She took us to France, one time, it was the only trip we ever made together."

Roland is interested because this is new.

"We couldn't afford the cities so we stayed out in the country, at a dreary beach place on the Normandy coast, in a family hotel with bad food and smells in the hall. We didn't like it particularly because there was nothing for American children to do and it rained all the time. But one day when it rained we took a walk and we found this garden where an old man was growing sweet peas."

Now Roland may be listening—it is not clear—or he may be drinking his coffee and thinking about something else. In any event, Madeline falls silent, not out of discouragement but because she does not feel capable of describing what she saw that day: her mother bent in the garden, her face in a mass of lavender sweet peas.

"The man cut a big bunch and gave them to her, and when she opened her purse to pay, he waved it away. And then," Madeline says, and now she is talking to herself, "she cried."

Ordinarily she would have added that her father had been

gone for a long time, that her mother had no friends in France, that the boys were being difficult, but now these explanations seemed irrelevant. The sequence—her mother burying her face in the flowers, the man giving her a bunch, her tears—is enough. No interpretation is needed.

"I'll be back in just a moment," Madeline says, getting up and almost falling over the knees of the man at the next table. She expects Roland to ask her where she's going but he says nothing and she finds herself oaring her way through the hot, fume-laden air.

It occurs to her that perhaps the florist's stall was a dream, that it will have vanished like the witch's hut in a fairy tale, but there it is, prosaically occupying its few feet of the sidewalk.

She heads straight for the tub of lavender sweet peas and seizes a bunch—yes, seizes, that is the word. Then she smells them to make sure the scent is there—it is—and hurries to the counter to pay. The sweet peas cost, as she quickly figures, five dollars in American money; she counts out the change and refuses the woman's offer of a paper to wrap the stems in. She barely notices the woman which is strange since all during their trip she has been recording every detail.

She is remembering the way her mother's pretty face crumpled. Madeline was only twelve when that happened, and she thinks at first she had been embarrassed—she must have been embarrassed!—but then she knows with certainty that she had not been embarrassed, that she had felt for her mother at that moment, and perhaps only at that moment, love.

For of course there had been disagreements later and separations and they had both faced each other finally like knights on horseback, holding their lances and shields.

Now Madeline sits down at the table and Roland glances at her as she holds out the bouquet. "I bought myself some sweet peas," she says, and tries to remember whether she has ever bought herself anything before. Of course she has, she is comfortably off, she has bought acres of clothes and furniture and dishes over the years, yet somehow that is not the same and she knows it is not the same because all those things had no link to love.

"Smell them," she says, and wonders again if she's ever said anything so direct. Roland leans forward a little and sniffs the bouquet.

"That was the only time I ever saw my mother cry," she reminds him, and a dry choking starts in her throat as though something is lodged there.

"Yes," he says, patiently.

She draws the flowers in close, inhaling their scent. "I never told you I loved her then," she says, "just the way I love you now. My two loves," she adds.

"That's nice," Roland says.

Now she knows what she wants to ask. "Why didn't you buy me the sweet peas?"

"I didn't think of it," he says.

"What do you think about?" she asks, gliding into deep, cold water.

"What kind of a question . . ."

"No kind of a question," she says. "I don't know if you love me."

"You know I do."

"No, I don't know," she says, and she shifts the sweet peas to her other hand. Their stems are growing warm, she doesn't know how she will preserve them.

"Well, I've told you," he says, and she looks at his beautiful face, the brown eyes she adores, the pallor and the charm that will always win him the hearts of women. "Yes, you've told me," she says, "but I've never believed it."

"Maybe you should wonder why."

She weighs that carefully, staring at the way the sweet pea blossoms are fastened, fragilely, to each stalk. Perhaps she caught her mother's sadness long ago, like a germ.

But finally she says, "I don't believe it because it isn't so," and the cafe and the city around it drop away.

THAT SENTENCE HAS FREED HER not from Roland—she never wanted to lose him—but from the tyranny of the past. She has loved twice in her life, and lost twice. She loved her mother, once, and the rest of what passed between them is irrelevant; yes, she loved Roland, she will probably always love him, and the fact that they do not see each other is irrelevant.

The sweet peas, of course, did not last through that long hot day.

The Author

Sallie Bingham published her first novel with Houghton Mifflin in 1961. Since then she has published four collections of short stories (including *Transgressions,* Sarabande Books, 2002), four novels, and a memoir. She was Book Editor for *The Courier-Journal* in Louisville and has been a director of the National Book Critics Circle. She is the founder of The Kentucky Foundation for Women.